TOO MUCH, TOO SOON

BY DAVID STOKES

PITTSBURGH, PENNSYLVANIA 15222

ISBN: 978-0-8059-8778-2
Printed in the United States of America

First Printing

For more information or to order additional books, please contact:
RoseDog Books
701 Smithfield Street
Third Floor
Pittsburgh, Pennsylvania 15222
U.S.A.
1-800-834-1803
www.rosedogbookstore.com

TOO MUCH, TOO SOON

On Oct. 25, 1965. A cold day, in Baltimore, MD; I was born into this measly little world; as far as I could remember at age 5. I was a very thin and sickly individual with nothing but love in my heart. I couldn't understand why people fight, kill, hate, break-up and make-up so much, out of all this pain and frustration come the story of Geneva stokes "yes" my mother, she done all for everyone and everybody. It was not a day that she was not going to the store, food market, or school for her friends or family members a like, my grandmother didn't feel the need to protect, provide, or care for my mother as she did my mother youngest and only sister Rose Stokes. Rosie was a mean streak; if anybody could be call the devil it was her, she had Gregory and Cookie to feed but she felt no need to feed them, Rose ran the street, stole, and raise sand day and night which put the weight on my (mother) Geneva Stokes shoulder, well mom had me, Lorene, Ben, Bernard, Genevieve, Daryl, Teresa, and Luther Stokes, to take care of. I was the second child, I sort of think I took after my mother although I was not spiritual at the time I sort of felt the Godly love my mother held for every one, she was truly a Good Samaritan. My father (POP) was an entirely different story. he was fresh out of prison Aug. 1972., real hot temper and quick with his fist, from a young child view, he was a monster, who didn't like no one, he also had a penchant for beating me, I try to rationalize that I was bad or did something wrong. as I look back over the years, I truly think he was afraid that I turn out to be better than him, POP always stated that his father used to beat him all the time, today I tell myself it made me tough, it help me to get through some of the hard

1

time in my life, such as prison and to lead my own gang with all that said and done I could live with that but if truth be told, life as a child was very traumatizing for me. I started elementary school at # 102 Thomas G. Hayes. the first day of school was a very exciting and a good day, but it was short lived. When K. K. slap me up side the head for no apparent reason, I was so hurt. than in the third grade Darren Purcell hit me in the chest and kick me in the back, I should had know every one was watching, I just cried, every day some one was slapping me around, I just beg, ran, and cried. One have to wonder what effect this was having on a seven years old kid. first of all I was getting tore to pieces from my father and big brother at home, and from the children at school. I sometime wonder where was God at these trouble times. when I was eight years old I talked to my mother she stated you are good at school. they're just jealous, which was a true enough statement. at this time I was getting straight "A", and I knew my time table 1-12 better than any body in the class. all I did was joke, laugh, and smile all the time, I truly couldn't understand why every body want to pick on me. Like Smokey Robinson stated there is nothing more sadder than the tear of a clown. One day at the age 9, my father beat me very brutally with an extension cord, it cut into my flesh, my back, legs, and buttock was cover with welt. I couldn't sit down in school the next day. I never told or shown the teacher, I just refuse to sit and I refuse to cooperate that day. My dad must to had been effective by the Vietnam war, may be agent orange and from what I Heard he had a very abuses father, one can only pity this man. my dad was a Vietnam Veteran with emotional problem, with a record a mile long for stealing and robbing. he was a very poor role-model, in home but not active, we were so poor my mother use to always go to Thrift and Second Hand Store our favor was located on North Ave. and Harford road "Veteran Warehouse, A.K.A. Little Sear we didn't contemplate going to Big Sear or any other store on Harford road/ North Ave. one time I Bought these orange shoe from Pick A Pair {Old Town Mall}, every body call them boats and clown shoe. they said you sure enough pick a pair that time. my mother was doing all the chore around the house, the pain and suffering was in her face, so much that a man by the name Robert Lee took notice and told her he would marry her and take care of all her children, well we liked him, he was a good father Image, no fussing, no cursing from him. just love from him. now my father found out, all these event lead unto me making my first prayer to the Lord. one day he beat my mother with a belt, all I could do is hear her holler and scream. I than fell to my knee and beg and pray to the Lord please don't let him kill her. that didn't change my mom. she still did for every one and she still loved unconditionally. at one point she gave her mother her pay check 4 time in a row. I couldn't understand her plight. but at a very young age I knew I got to do something some day. than in the fifth grade at a basketball game, I met this young girl who always sat next to me in class. 3 weeks later one of my male classmate beat both of us up. as I stated I was getting a triple dose of pain, school, my father, and from Ben(my oldest brother). I couldn't understand Ben he was the oldest much bigger and stronger than I. he couldn't or wouldn't fight or pick with no body on the street neither did he fight my battle, I mean it was some guy his age in the same grade, sometime the same class picking and beating on me. Ben didn't say a word, nor did he lift a hand let a lone a finger. my mother had Ben by another lover and he came out dark skinned, black like his father. my father was brown skin so I came out light skinned. my brother (Ben) must have gotten a hold of one of William(Willie)Lynch book. because he sure had that mentality, Willie did a good job at dividing, he was struck on divide and conquer, he formulate a plan to treat one shade of color different. such as keep the light skin(brothers)slave in the house as a house Negroes, put the much darker Negroes in the (field) sun as a field Negro, also he always throw a few extras to a slave. when all was said and done, Willie than have a network of spy, snitcher, back stabber and (Police) if a slave could be call that. this was sheer manipulation on Willie Lynch behalf, also this method prove to be good on many occasion, Willie could be in town and he know what was said and done in his absent, this squash many uprising before it had a chance to formulated or start. Willie move quickly, precisely, brutally, and forcefully to stop revolt. right to this very day, the darker brothers and darker sisters can't stand the lighter brothers and sisters, this apply to the family as well as the street brothers and sisters. Willie Lynch was so famous for his technique and book. you got people of all color and nations reading, teaching, preaching, and practicing his technique, method, and teaching. they read his book back in the 1800. they really started hanging and Lynching black, also they form what became known as the Lynch mob. But if me and Ben would had struck together, we could have ran the project, who could go up against to mean fighting brothers, people would have thought twice or 3 time before crossing or picking with one of us, because we would had have each other back, you mess with one, these other was sure enough to come after you, sometime both could have been on some body ass. a regular Frank and Jesse James, But this wasn't to be the case, all Ben wanted to do is fight me. Now in the fifth grade at another basketball game, big Darren Purcell whom tormented me in the third grade, had in mind I was fair game and easy picking, because there were never nothing to fear from me, there wasn't an ounce of retaliation or fight coming from me, But this very day Darren Purcell got the shock and surprise of his life, Because on this day I develop a bond with the most notorious youngster whom ever crawl from his mother womb to reign terror at school #102 (Thomas G. Hayes). Bobby Johnson would be describe as a Mike Tyson, Ray Lewis killing machine, he was brown skin, with thick chest, big arms and walked with a swagger, he had this way how he addressed and talked to people that most didn't even think about challenging him, he was so fast and quick with his fist, so fast that you were hit 3 time before you could said hello, Bobby Johnson was quick, fast, hard, and strong. which earned him his leadership quality, he played football, baseball, and basketball, female just loved him. he talked like he was Humphrey Bogart, and walked with a bop, so bow legged that he stood on his hind legs and struck down his victim like a cobra, he was of average height, he look at you with these mean eyes that belied his youth, he had the build and body that spoke of strength, he was truly a fighting machine, the way he walk and talk demand and command respect. he had an air and aura of authority. On this particular day Bobby Johnson reputation proceeded him. Bobby Johnson told Darren Purcell to leave me alone, Darren and Bobby stood toe to toe, pound for pound. you have to know Darren was no slouch in the fight game. and right to this day I could still see the gleam in Bobby eyes as he rose to accept the challenge. Darren started off with an over hand right, follow with a left hand uppercut, both blow miss Bobby pivot on his right foot and let out a volley of 3 shot to the head, Darren stagger but didn't go down, Darren in return caught Bobby with a straight hard right, that any lesser man would have been down, But Bobby than proceed to throw a flurry of blow that rain down on Darren jaw, head, and chin. Darren looked shook and perhaps hurt, but he just dance away from Bobby, only to do some fancy footwork and deliver a solid blow to Bobby chin, Bobby head snap back, it seems bobby was

4

more mad than hurt, so Bobby change his tactic, He hit Darren with a devastating blow to the stomach, Darren air just left his body like a deflated tire, and he made the final mistake of dropping his guard to grab his aching stomach and was met by a solid right to the nose, which produce a flow of blood, like a river flow. Darren let out a scream and drop to one knee with both hands in the air a sure sign of true defeat and surrendering. As I stated from this day on there were a bond form between me and Bobby Johnson, we were thick as thieves, other jointed this little crew soon we had a big gang under the leadership of Bobby. There were many who felt under the feet, hands and boots of this notorious school age gang. All the while it was heaven sent for a young fifth grader whom didn't know a thing about hand to hand combat. Than in the six grade, we had our graduation party, they play (memory) = the way we were =, and Diana Ross (Supremes) reach out and touch somebody hand. We all shook hands and I said good bye Bobby. When I listen to the radio and hear Bill Withers sing lean on me and Aretha Franklin sing Respect, I often think of Bobby Johnson. Now time was moving much to fast, I found myself in the seventh grade at Lombard Jr. High School, at age 12, I was real bright and smart, a little green far as street knowledge was concern, but I never could be called yellow no more, So that's one of the many reason I enter a fight many simply said I had nothing to do with. What every body didn't know I had a selfish motive and a secret direct interest in recruiting this up and coming young gangster. First of all I must say it was very funny how the whole demonstration kick off Little Charles Nelson was sitting at the classroom table counting his funds, he claim he took 4,500 when he made a quick hustle the night before, every body including me that knew Charles Nelson, also knew without a shadow of doubt, that some body was short of 4,500. Because little Nelson was no joke when it came to robbing and stealing. But he was never much good with his hands otherwise. So as he was counting his ill-gotten gain, this guy in the class named Ricky Ford approached him and stated nigger I will beat your ass and take all your money. 1 guess at this time Charles Nelson didn't want to be relief of his hard earned cash. So when Ricky Ford stepped to him, Charles put his money in his pocket and fought back real hard, But it was a losing Battle for Charles Nelson, for Ricky Ford was much bigger, taller, stronger, and tougher with a mean right jab. After Charles Nelson caught two of those solid right jabs. I knew it was time for me to intervene and put my plan into action, First of all philosophically I knew Charles Nelson was a walking bank, and money making machine, Yes he had a way of making a quick buck. With my luck, my poor family position and possession which wasn't much. Could and would be greatly influence if I win Little Charles Nelson confident and friendship. As it stood this was my greatest opportunity to bring Charles Nelson abroad. So I couldn't be any more bless than when Ricky ford stepped to Charles. Well as the fight continue and I saw Ricky Ford pulverizing little Charles Nelson. I said pick on somebody your size, Ricky Ford than turn his full attention on me, so we squared off, I let him throw the first blow, He committed himself to a good butt whipping that very day, because when he open up with that weak blow, I lash out with a 19 piece blows all straight solid shots to the head and face, I dropped him like a bad habit, little Charles Nelson thanked me, and we jointed forces. Little did I know this was to lead me down a very foul, violent, dangerous and self destructive road. I truly enter a race and dance with the Devil. Because this little Negro introduce and expose me to a life of crime. People had look at us as an odd couple, 1 was fairly handsome, and Charles Nelson was short and ugly. But to me his skill, talent, and uncanny ability of making that dollar bill truly made up for his shorts coming, I guess in every body eyesight Charles Nelson was little short and stocky and looked like a troll and a midget. "Yes", ugly was not the word, Tore up from the floor up would be more accurate, Charles Nelson had a little boy body with an old man face. He had 12 brothers and sisters, father was a Preacher, Charles swore he could run basketball and box, But I seen better. Charles Nelson could draws real good, but he was a little average intelligent, He had the heart of gold, would give me, my family and his so called girlfriends any thing. Charles Nelson looked, walked, and acted like a gorilla. He had just a little fight in him. He had a way of seizing people up and than looking for my help. He was truly my shadow. Charles Nelson looked like a modern day cave man. He could be called Donky Kong Jr. Any way Charles Nelson introduce me to Steve Richards. Together we were 3 young crooks. One summer day we broke into Mack's clothing store, we took every thing. I said take every thing to my house. Than we took off 6 more stores. Once again I stated take every thing to my place. Than we rob a jewelry store I resigned to my favor statement take every thing to my house. Steve Richards started to cut his eye at me, also look at me out the corner of his eye at me. I truly

6

didn't take the look on Steve Richards face as a threat or could I said a future threat. But as time when on I heard from Charles Nelson and the street grapevine that Steve Richards was not to happy about me always taking stuff over my house and me and my family getting the bulk of every thing. I must said I wasn't truly mad because for one, it was true, and the other reason was that I already knew there will always be time when one will come along and try to challenge your leadership. I chalk it up as one of those things. We use to hit the bread, meat, milk, and insurance man. Also we were committing so many (B-n-E)= Breaking and Entering. Me, Charles Nelson and Steve Richards broke into this appliance store, we took TV., radio, phone and other electrical device. We were now taking down 20 store a month and every thing when to my house again. The fruit man and insurance man caught total hell, after they collected their bill money we were waiting. I scoped out a store that fix, repair, and sold new watches, it was next on my list, we broke into it at 4 o'clock in the morning. The funny thing was, it was a store that sold watches, but no one was watching us. Three weeks later I was walking with 4 other dudes, one of them named Terrell was talking to me about how he heard that I was getting money and he want to get paid too. As I was crossing one of the busy street in East Baltimore (Orleans Street), I saw this white man with a business suit on and for no apparent reason I told the white man I should rob you. I was so busy turning my head looking at the white man, that I step into the intersection and was hit by a car fill with 4 white women. The car just nip me on the right leg, because of my quick reflect I was able to jump on top of the car before it really connected with me. I got off the hood in look inside of the car, I was shock and surprise at what I saw, or better still, whom I saw in the car, it was 4 nuns they had on their black Habit. I thought to myself was this God trying to tell me something. What ever the case, At that point I wasn't "Ready to Receive". The Nuns looked at me and said was I alright? I said "yes". Than Terrell lean over and he whisper in my ear lets snatch their pocketbook I said no. So we walked away and the 4 Nuns drove off. When I got home, I told my mother she stated you alright? Did you get names, address, phone numbers, and their license plate number? I said no, I'm alright. She said you might not feel it now but later on. Also it could effect you years later. Looking back I truly think she just wanted to sue, I was too young to know about Lawsuit or at lease I was never expose to it back than. I remember time when

I was over West-B-More and came home to Latrobe Project which was over East-B-More, stuff was stack up I mean cartons of cigarette, cases of soda, meats, fruits, eggs, breads, jewelry and other can goods all pile and stack up against the wall in my house. Yes, my boys truly look out for me even when I wasn't present. Well when I came home from the West side my parent would hit me and say you're punish. But that never stop them from accepting the ill-gotten merchandise. I often said to myself I wasn't even home, how the stuff get in the house. We started taking down a lot more Jewelry and clothing store, as the old statement goes take every thing back to my house. Again Steve Richards was starting to show his true color. I know people could see and feel the animosity growing between us. But he could never be a true leader, for one thing little Charles Nelson and the rest of the guy didn't respect him or look up to him like they did me. Never-the-less, I was ready to step to him. But things cooled down, there were a lot of money to be made, I mean me, Charles Nelson, and Steve Richards were robbing, stealing, and breaking into every thing. We were up 3 and 4 o'clock in the morning. Last to go to bed, first to get up. One day we broke into this school, we all got caught. Since we were juvenile they took each of us to our parents. When the police knocked on the door, my father answer it, he said yes sir officers, the 3 officers came in with me, they begin to tell my parent what I did, But before the 3 Officers could finish, my father hit me 3 time in the face, grab my collar, threw me on the floor start hitting, kicking, and stomping me. All the long shouting I got this. You don't be stealing or breaking into any thing. Yes sir officers I got this. The 3 officers let this action go on for about 2 minute. (Because back than the Child Abuse law was not really enforced.) The officers were now laughing when my dad proceeded to drag me across the floor by one leg. This Uncle Tom Ass Nigger was all I could think. One of the officer smiled and pat my father on the back (as if to say good boy). But instead the office said don't kill him, than the 3 officers left. I resume getting money on one particular day my (little baby brother) Luther Stokes, stated he was tired of me giving him money, clothes, food and Jewelry etc. So I said, go on a hustle with me, he said let call your boys, I said no, I wanted to be the first one to show him how to get a few dollars. So we when out together and I stuck up this Insurance man. Luther was delight by all the dough I made off this one little hustle, also this was his first, and he was much please, he told me as much, me and him when on 5 more hustle alone. He was what you could call lock, stock, sold, and bought. 2 day later I was arrested for a robbery. They detain me at the station house. When I came home, Luther and I when on 2 more robbery. Luther stated (Dave) you are a thorough nigger and to top it off you are my only big brother. I said wait a minute, I'm next to the oldest, you do have a big brother, but it not me, I was thinking all the boys in our family have the same mother, even our big brother, we never had a step brother. So how could he stand there and call me his only big brother, (not that I was mad). Than he broke it down to me, he stated I call you my only big brother, because you are my true big brother, my real big brother (Ben) is a sucker, he greener than a pool table and twice as square, he a real live coon, he never did any thing wrong or right, he never been to jail, he never help neither of us out, it away been me and you, let keep it that way. I said he still our big brother. Luther said all Ben do is stay home and bully every body around the house including mom. So I finally accepted the fact that I was his big brother in his eyesight. Now my little brother was part of the gang. Steve Richards, Charles Nelson, Luther and I. Were now hanging to together. We had a string of device and vice of getting money. We broke into cars, stores, houses, and schools. We even stole from big food chain such as Super Pride located over East-B-More on Chase and Patterson Park, we even use to be by the rail road tracks in back of Super Pride, waiting for their trucks to unload. Luther Stokes started his own little gang, they were getting paid. One day me, Steve Richards and Charles Nelson when to the store (Two Guys) which was Located on Belair Road, we went out there to steal some Glue (Kuiee). We have now began huffing, puffing, and sniffing Glue, our gang would tear a mattress apart, sometime we found an old mattress by the dumpster, or we even when as far as destroying and tearing our own bed apart just for the cotton, we wet the cotton with the (Kuiee) Glue, than you sniff and huff it, we call it catching a dream, it was nothing to hear some body say give me a wet one, or I need a wet one, they even might say let me buy a wet one from you. The whole Latrobe Project was doing this in the "70". Not knowing it was destroying our brain cell which cause brain damage, for (Kuiee) was nothing more than (paint thinner) a form of turpentine, it left you with bad breath, peeling fingers and hand, sometime a bad headaches, with a nasty taste in your mouth, and you just kept on hawk spitting and left your house stinking like elbow Jenking, we also use to cry easy when people that didn't sniff or huff pour it out, or when one of us get mad at the other Glue Sniff-er and pour the glue out of the can, I mean when you see that red and white can of (Kuiee) Glue up side down with no cap or top on it and some body holding it over the sink, toilet, or ground dumping it out we would start trying to fight, kill, scream, and go crazy, than cry when the can is empty. (Two Guys) store and this (Hardware) store on Monument and Patterson Park got paid off the sale of this paint thinner (Glue) = Kuiee. This is why Me, Steve Richards, and Charles Nelson found our self at Two Guys, we were going to steal some Glue, but other people from all over must to have been sniffing Glue also, or at lease some body from Latrobe Project must had beat us there, it wasn't a single can there, so we stole this big can of other stuff because it was in a red and white can like the Glue we were known for. This other stuff was in a can twice as bigger than our Glue we sniff. We each put one can in our underwear and walked out the store. If the can was open, we would have been much more careful when we put it in our underwear. Because if this Glue spill on your penis, you would want some body to call the fire department (no not literally) it don't put you on fire. The Kuiee Glue just feel like hot water when it hit the balls and penis. The hairs on your testicle and your genital organ feel like hot oil was pour on you, But since we were at a store thus fore the cans were sealed there-fore we put the big can in our under-wear and made it out side, when we open one can we didn't like what we saw, so we open the remaining two can, it held this real thick white stuff, we pull out our cotton wet it and put this new and unfa-miliar stuff to our nose to get high but nothing happen. We than threw the can against the wall. Our Glue don't smell or look like that, it not thick at all, it not even what you could call Glue, in-fact when most people hear the word Glue, they automatically associate this with the Glue we use in Elementary School, the Glue we use to huff, puff, and sniff was thin, in a can and in a liquid form, that why they call it paint thinner. (I kept mine in a Pepsi bottle). After toss-ing the unwanted cans against the wall, than against my better judg-ment and the warming bell going off in my head, we when back in (Two Guys) Department store. We pocket a lot of un-paid for mer-chandise, my coat and pant pockets were about to burst from the steam, as we were heading out the store, we were stop by two store security guards, they escorted Me, Charles Nelson, and Steve Richards toward a back room, they didn't handcuff us, so as we walk down the aisle I was un-loading my pockets, I was secretly putting stuff on any shelf in arm reach, they took us to this office, and stated you know the 3 of you should be in school, there fore in-violation of the Curfew Laws, now empty your pockets, much to my surprise, Steve Richards and Charles Nelson still had all of their stolen goods in their pocket, I than spoke up and said Officers you can see that I don't have nothing, I proceed to pat and turn my coat and pant pockets inside out, and said you can even check me. One officer pointed to the floor, by my feet was one AA side battery, I said wait a minute that was already there, that not even a 9 volt battery, what I need or what can I do with just one battery. The officer said that your battery. Before I could further complaint, the officer ask us have we been arrested for shoplifting before? We stated no sir. He said I'm not going to arrest any body and I'm not going to call the police, I just want to take all 3 of your photo, so we can know if you 3 come out here to steal again. The 2 officers than walk us to the back of the room, I saw the camera, and thousand of photo all on the desk, floor, and wall. As I took a closer look, I saw some familiar faces, so we agree to have our photo taken, the officer took out photo and ask for our name, D.O.B., 7 digits, and address to attach to the photo.(right to this very day) I wonder what happen to all those thousand of photo they sure didn't return mine. The security guards let us go home. 2 day later Me and the gang including my little brother Luther stokes when up to Fair Mount Hill and Patterson Park to make some money, we rob two Paper Boys. Than we seen 3 white boy, they were standing on a hill. We approach and surrounded them and said don't move, don't run. We begin to check their pocket, they have a pocket full of money, a pack of Top papers and marijuana this was some colorful top papers (all colors) and when I put a joint (J) to my mouth, the favors of this Top papers was sweet, this made me smoke 5 more J.. So we turn to walk away, before we could make it across the hill, about 25 Caucasian came down the street, the other 3 white boys we just rob call out to them, hey these niggers just rob us. The crowd came walking fast. Luther Stokes tripped and was rolling half way down the hill where the 25 or so white boys were waiting. I grab him and we ran back up the hill. Right to this day I don't know why those 25 or more white boys didn't chase us, I think GOD was to be credit for this or maybe they didn't know what we had in our pocket. But I knew the latter was nonsense because we didn't display any weapon when we rob the 3 white boys. And we didn't shoot or show no gun when the 25 or so white boys came, also we ran, So I knew it was GOD. Once again "I wasn't ready to receive". We than made it back to the Project. When we reached Latrobe. There were 8 police cars park. I said to myself they must be looking for us, every body in the gang must to have been feeling and thinking the same thing, because some body said damn, another said oh shit. Every body said let split up, we will meet later if nothing happen. So we departed, I than when in the house, to my surprise there were no cops present, and my family didn't seem if any thing was amiss, so I relax, But I was still puzzle why so many police cars, Yes the Project was bad and things happen daily, But one still want to know what going on in his neighborhood. 10 minute when by and finally came an answer to all my questions, Luther stokes came in the house, he told me that the police wasn't looking for us. 1 said I already know that. Than Luther said that nigger Eric Rowe is cruddy, people outside said he just rob and hurt this 75 years old white women while she was waiting on the bus stop. He beat her unconsciously and took her pocketbook. People said if she was black they would have stopped him. I said is he lockup? Luther said no, because no one told on him. But the Ambulance came for her. I said we must to have missed the Ambulance truck. Because it was nothing but police cars out there when we reached the Project. Luther stokes said but there is a large puddle of blood out there, she must to have been really hurt. Luther said I hope she don't die, I said me to. Luther than said Eric Rowe is crazy. The next day Me and my gang broke into the bread and meat truck and we was selling breads and meats to the whole neighborhood. After this food, breads and money ran out, I tried a new hustle, we hit the Green W.I.C. truck. We had eggs, cereal, milk, and frozen orange juice for sale. I heard many baby crying and wailing through out the Project especially at night, there was so much crying, screaming, hollering, and wailing from the hungry children that I couldn't sleep. So I didn't try this hustle again. One day my father came to me and said it getting to hot for you over here. He also said he got a brother that live in West Baltimore (Park Heights/Green Spring) Apartment, so I went there to stay a while. Without my father blessing I shown little Charles Nelson how to get out there. My father was piss. One Summer day while Me and Charles Nelson was out there, Charles Nelson got into some shit, He had a few words with a dude name Jason. This was the last thing I needed or wanted, for one, Jason had a gang that ran Green Spring Apartments. This was safe Haven for me. I knew I shouldn't have shown Charles Nelson my where about. Now we were beefing with one of the most notorious gang in Park Heights. One tale that stood out in my mind was how they jump this guy named Glenn Weiner, they caught him in the basement laundry room. They came in the front and back door of the Apartment Building, Glenn Weiner was down the basement washing clothes. They broke his nose, jaw, and kick all of his front tooth out. When I saw little Charles Nelson and Jason arguing over this female, I told Jason to step off. He did, but in the back of my mind I knew I hadn't seen or heard the last of this. 4 days pass and nothing happen. So we got careless. On the 5 day my prediction came true.

Me and Charles Nelson were sitting on my uncle old car, they came from all 4 directions East, West, North, and South, they even came through the back door of the Apartment they had us trap. So they move in close Quarter and surrounded us. That when Jason ask Charles Nelson to repeat what he said a few days ago. Before I knew it Jason and them started hitting and kicking Charles Nelson, they Ignore me. As Charles Nelson when into the building they beat him on the steps they beat, kick, and punched him all the way to the top floor where my Uncle lived, this continue until I enter the building. 2 dudes follow me up the stairs, But no one touch me. Than they retreated and left the building. As I let Charles Nelson in the apartment I felt bad But lucky, the next day I told my uncle and he stated you're going to fight them one by one But wait until I come from work. That morning my uncle when to work, me and Charles Nelson was on my uncle balcony, Jason and 15 of his gang member came walking down the street, they were outside standing like they own the street, they holler up to us, come on outside, I said not now but 4:30 sharp. They laugh and said he trying to sound like a business man. My uncle came home at 4:25 pm. And we left the house to keep this much dreaded appointment. We spotted them in front of the only building that held a swimming pool at Green Spring Apartment. Jason gang and us met each other half way, I said I wanted Jason, But Jason when straight at Charles Nelson. Gordon (the Leader) stepped to me. He took a karate stand which sort of shook me up, because I never done karate, or fought any body who knew karate, the gang bum-rush Charles nelson, all hell broke loose. My Uncle stated don't bank him. " one on one " these cats started doing

13

karate kicks, screaming, jumping and flying through the air, my uncle had no choice but to back off, for he was a grown man, and we were merely teenager, this was back in 1978. West B-more, especially park heights was famous for karate. Back in 1978, Bruce Lee was showing in every movies theater, it was the trend, every teenager stated I'm going to the Apollo on Harford road. Which shown 2 karate movies for 50 cents, me and my gang use to go to Virginia bakery on Harford road pay them 25 cents for a big bag of doughnut also this Virginia bakery believe in selling fresh dough-nut after the end of the day what ever they didn't sell they gave away in the back of the shop, we use to battle for those doughnut than we use to had so many dough-nut that we threw them at one another like snow ball. Any how this bakery caught fire and every body claim Virginia bakery on Harford road was burn down for Insurance policy. But we still when to The Apollo on Harford road to see karate flick, back in 1978 it was nothing to hear some body said they were going down-town to the Mayfair, Town, the New, or Hippodrome movie theater to see a karate flick, mainly Bruce Lee. Any way as me and Gordon did battle. I got mad when he kick me in the chest for the fifth time, I fake like I was going to guard my chest, I than threw one solid blow, that connected with the Leader (Gordon) head, it produce a loud bang on contact, Gordon knee buckle, his guards drop and his eyes roll back in his head, every body said "whew" it took Gordon one minute and some second to get himself together. Than he kick me in the chest. My uncle broke it up. When we got back to my uncle apartment, my uncle said Dave if you would had follow up you would have knock him out. That night me and Charles Nelson was in the woods which was directly behind the Green Spring Apartment, when Jason, Gordon and their gang came into the woods, I said to myself not again, But much to my surprise they said we fought well and we have heart, than we all shook hands. Than Charles Nelson and I walked to Latrobe Project. One night in 1979 we when down Old Town Mall and broke into a Chinese store, the police caught Charles Nelson, Steve Richards, and 3 of the other gang member. You see this would have never had happen if we didn't make 4 trips back and forth carrying all the merchandise back to my place 917 Wilmot Court (Latrobe Project). We were on our fifth trips, I stop to speak to this female, the rest of the gang proceeded to go into the store, I saw about 4 police cars pull up, Right to this day I think some body from Dollar House Alley call the police.

Dollar House Alley is located behind Old town mall, you pay one Dollar to move in but spend Hundred, thousand, and perhaps million to fix the house up. When I saw the police cars, I ran home. I had all the luxury, Jewelry, money, watches, clothes, and radio to myself, But I felt truly hurt, my whole gang gone in one blow, But I was even much more hurt the next day when I receive a call from (Hickey School) Training School, Charles Nelson told me that Steve Richards was going to snitch on me. 2 weeks later word on the street was that Charles Nelson had Steve Richards raped in Training School. I started staying home with my mother, and going over my grandmother house, My mom mother was my favor grandmother, although I loved all my grandmother, she was my heart, my grandmother Ms Stokes did for every body, people use and abuse her, this must be where my mother got her good conduct from. My mother and grandma (Ms Stokes) use to read the Bible. My grandma called me China Boy. I use to look into the mirror to see why she call me that. One day I ask her, I said my eyes are not slanted, and I don't speak Chinese, Why do you call me China Boy? She said you're not like Ben, Teresa, Lorene, or none of them, you are always up when my company come, you make sure I'm safe. My Grandmother loved to cook and she could cook. In July 1980 I cried. (Ms Stokes) my grandmother died. On the day she died, it pour down rain. people stated that mean she when to heaven. The doctor said she had a large heart with a hole in it. After her funeral, which was my first funeral I attend and I didn't understand the wake. People were dancing, singing, partying, hugging, kissing, eating, drinking, telling joke and playing fast music. I ask myself what going on here, my favor grandma was bury today. Well 3 day before my grandmother died a bird flew in my parents house (917 Wilmot Court). It flew in my mom and dad room, they thought they ran it out, But when they open the window the next day it flew out. My mother and father woke me, my brothers, and sisters up, got all of us together in the living room and told us about the bird. They said when a bird fly in some body house it mean death. We than walk over my grandmother house, all of us when to 801 McAleer Court and knock my grandmother answer the door. My mother told her what happen, my grandma than also said it mean death, than she said China Boy is going to be all right. Although I was breaking every laws and getting into trouble I didn't understand why she said this. After my favor grandma pass I was frustrated, also my whole gang was serving time

15

at Hickey School, I truly missed my right hand man little Charles Nelson, but as the saying goes, one monkey don't stop no show. No disrespect to my comrade, but I had to move on, and I had to eat also. Really at this point I was very vulnerable which meant I could be easily persuaded and easily Influence. I let a much weaker and dim-witted person mislead me. I don't know what I was thinking. I let this dim-witted soul Eric Rowe expose me to snatching pocket-book, I grab one pocketbook, Eric Rowe snatch several, one particular day he snatch an old lady pocketbook while I was urinating in an alley. When the police came, they stated, you were in Eric Rowe present. Therefore we are charging both of you, plus I had a record and didn't go to school. They sent Eric Rowe to Montrose, I couldn't believe it, the Court sent Eric Rowe to Montrose where girls where committed also. They sent me to Training School For Boys, So Dec. 1980 I enter Maryland Training School. I was sort of scare and nervous, I knew more about getting money than fighting, so I told myself, I'm going to build up my Reps. I guess I was thinking philosophically, when you swim with sharks, you got to show your teeth. I also remember Bobby Johnson, if it didn't teach me nothing else, it demonstrated you got to be hard, command and demand respect, take what yours. I guess in this world you learn early on, respect is simply just not giving, you must earn it, if some body have to be on the business end of your fist so be it. Well my first 12 fights I beat hand down, I could recall one particular fight, I hit this cat whom thought he was a smooth fighter, I hit him with a 25 piece blow. That when all the staff members and other Juvenile stated I should be a boxer, most thought I use to Box. Also I used to lift weights while every body else ran ball. I truly pick up a bad habit. I learned to choke my Chicken — masturbation, I called my right hand Ms. Five, one night I was playing spade, and the baddest Juvenile Delinquent in my cottage, was saying things that just didn't sound right, he was indirectly trying me. It is said if a person chump you down with their mouth half the battle is won already. This cat was Kevin Stanley from D.C., These D.C. Joe, or D.C. Yo Thought they were Sugar Ray Leonard although Sugar Ray Leonard came from Palmer Park Maryland, Back in the 1980 Sugar Ray was King of the ring, so every D.C. Joe try to claim him and be him. I wanted Kevin Stanley to know B-More, Meant Be More careful. But as I sat at the table playing cards, Kevin Stanley Kept selling Death. I than said man for real, We can bypass all that mother fucking rap, we both jump up, threw down the cards and both said what up at the same time? Than both started throwing blow, I caught him with a 12 piece blows, he was all up on the table. This is when I bond with an E-B-More dude by the name of Frank Brices. This nigger was about his work. they use to said check your self and bring you up for group meeting. But they never brought me or Frank Brices up. the group meeting were wild, whom ever they has said check yourself to the most were place in the middle of the circle, and every body screaming, cursing, fussing at them, I seen many Juvenile cry when put in this circle, this was mental, emotional, spiritual, and Psychological abuse. I cut into this Caucasian named Roy Dixson, he was very cool for a white boy, it was a new and rewarding experience, the hoods that I grew up in and hang around there was no white boys, this was my first exposure to them. They are not evil or bad as one would think. If one would or could imagine we all bleed, eat, shit, and die the same, it would be all right, I dig his style with a smile, He knew how to gamble, do 3 card monte, play chess, checker, and all sort of cards game. He looked and acted like John Gotti. And he had my back, as well as I had his. Me and Roy Dixson were even on the same football, Baseball, and Basketball team. These girls came from Montrose for a swimming pool party and his female cousin came on the bus and Roy Dixson hooked us up, I got my first kiss from a white chick that day and she wrote me as soon as she got back to Montrose. One summer day, Roy Dixson was fighting a D.C. (Joe) Mack Harvey busted Roy Dixson eye wide open, He cheated he hit Roy Dixson with a ring studded hand. I knocked him out for Roy Dixson, we had a gang fight that day. All the black staff member turn on me. One of the group leader staff stated you don't help no white boy against no black people. They are your natural foe. (this very act came back to haunt me years later). I was release from Training School in the summer of 1981. I was flying straight, or some could said I was walking straight, my main man Andrew mason was a cat fresh off the step, he was Physically bigger than me, but 2 years younger. I heard a little about him while I was in Training School, he made his bone, now he was looking to spread his wings. He already pull off a lot of heist and he stole cars. He pull me up 3 weeks after my stint up Training School, He stated he wanted to be down for me. Our first stick up together was an insurance man, we made 7 thousand dollars. after that we were robbing, stealing, and breaking in store and houses and he was a master car thief.

17

We also banded together so his enemy could be mine and my enemy his, one particular event had a lasting impression on my mind, Andrew mason called this girl Angie from my house, her boyfriend knock on my door and stated no disrespect to you Dave, But I want to see Andrew Mason, I said nigger you don't be knocking on my door for my nigger. We beat him up in the snow, we made him eat snow and we bury him in the snow, People outside was laughing. Well Andrew Mason, Charles Nelson, and myself had now hooked up and was robbing every thing that move, among us 3 we easily saw 200,000 back in 1981 that was a lot of money. But like all young hustler we spent every thing. As I recall, my house was the first to have a big color remote control TV. And VCR., every body else had Betamax, with Betamax, you could only get certain (tape) movies, Because there wasn't a wide variety of movies for Beta, also Betamax show a lot of weak movies. Than little Charles Nelson got lock up, he was committed to Montrose. So Andrew Mason and I had to carry on with our boy gone. I stole this long double barrel shot gun the kind the old farmer and old sheriff had and some people went hunting with, it was so big and long, that I couldn't tote the damn thing. My uncle Butch stated we should cut it down and that he have a hacksaw, so I saw a little, which left a split and slit in the barrel than I crawl on the roof, we use to had sun roof down Latrobe Project. You could climb on your bedroom door. Pull open the hatch in the ceiling and get on the roof, I got on the roof, I mistakenly held the shotgun by the slit and split in the barrel and fired it. It put a hole in my left hand middle finger. I was bleeding badly. I holler Butch., he ran out the house. In 1982 me and Andrew Mason made the foolish mistake of robbing an Caucasian Insurance man Down-Town, we were caught, by me being the oldest and most violent they sent Andrew Mason to Training School and they waive on me, sent me straight to the adult system, City jail, Court/ Steel side. I couldn't believe this stroke of bad luck. I was just turning 15. The court appointed me a Public Defender Mr. Bosley Katzenberg, He acted like he couldn't chew bubble gum and walk at the same time. As I waited over (B.C.J.) Baltimore City Jail 401 E. Eager Street. We when to school 740 with the women, one guy whole family was there (2 brothers and 1 sister). It wasn't t bad over there, we took picture, the Sun paper and the News America Paper feature a photo of us 740 School student, I was over the Annex trying to Adjust to the Therapeutic program, they made grown man parade around in diaper and sign that read I'm dumb and stupid and made you clean up floor and toilet with just a tooth brush pure Psychological abuse. They made sure we when to school, which was 740. We use to go through the tunnel which was a door next to the visiting room as we enter this tunnel we were directed to the roof were the female gym was held also this building contain the school building, some inmate completed their G.E.D. there. That why The Sun and News America paper was Interested with this particular section of Baltimore City Jail. Well the days spent at the jail was uneventful, nothing to raise an alarm. The Courts held a hearing concerning the matter about a motion of reverse waiver that was filed by me and my Public Pretender, (NO I didn't make a mistake). That should be their Legal name, because the jail and Penal System is fill with us when we use a Public Defender. I must confess to one thing I was truly hurt and shock about the report that Training School gave about me, they over stated their hand, they made me out to be a monster that was so foul and vile that only a long period of Incarceration in a maximum security prison could rehabilitate me. But if truth be told. I was just haunted by my past, mainly because I helped that Caucasian Roy Dixson. Well I was sentenced to 4 years in prison. I was only 15 years old, but my street smarts, toughness, confident, and Training School knowledge had me ready for any and every thing. I harden my heart, my soul turned cold, my first night there I saw this young guy get rape, the way he was screaming, begging, crying, pleading, and hollering cast off a sound that I will never forget, I was a little nervous, also I was one of the first from my hoods to go to an Adult Prison, back in 1982, 15 years old were not much waive on, they when to Training School or Montrose. The old men thought all young guy were dumb and green, especially fresh fishes, or so called new meat. They were placing bets, who was going to be the first to turn a young nigger out. One must understand prison is just a Society with in a Society. On the street an older man love to have a young big butt girl in his corner and will use any trick to get her, in prison there are many so called R-Kelly in all prison, there are no young female inmate, so they turn to the young boys inmate, to some man in prison it a form of respect, power, control, hardness, pride and joy, ego stroking notch on his belt. These kind of men said the greatest power is when they made a man suck one of his friend penis. It is nothing to see two man get married by a jail house preacher. I heard A lot of men in prison Quote there is no better joy than a big butt boy. It was sad to see men playing game on each other. One game play was to go to commissary (store) on your schedule day. Commissary store is unusually outside your housing unit tier. While you're in that long commissary line waiting to place your order, one inmate will approach you with several bags filled with grocery, said hey man can you watch these bags for me, I will be back in a minute, than he walk off. Than another inmate (his friend) approach you, said my man, my friend told me to collect his bags. You think it okay. So you give him the bags, than he walk off, But before you could get out of the line with your order, the first inmate come back and say where is my bags?. You say I gave them to your People. The first inmate will say I didn't sent or tell nobody to get my bags. This trick will leave you with the bill, the first inmate will hand you a big long list for you to recover at your own expense. If you don't pay up you will be knifed or get a lock in the sock upside the head or he will tell you get mine or be mine. I also knew the hounds would try me soon or later, so I mentally prepared myself for this moment of truth, and sure enough it came, in a form of an old head by the name rock, he made a hasty decision of seizing me up wrong. He was much bigger and perhaps stronger, he bent down 21 years, from what I gather he was in a few of the roughest prison including this one on several occasion, also he was a booty bandit, when he approach me, he wasn't to certain how to handle me, that gave me the edge I needed, he half-hearted try to grab me, I already had a shank for occasion just like this, so I stabbed him in the right eye, I put it out, no one snitch, they flew him out, from that day on it was smooth sailing for me, I earned some of the most harden and career criminal respect, now I wanted to stretch out and spread my wings. I joined a gang started running up in cell taking food, clothes, and jewelry. In my Philosophical mind you either handle or be handle, there were no two way about that, But I never could bring myself to rape nobody, I use to see a young inmate bend over, with a train of men in line, some of the men would call out come on Dave get some of this punk pussy, this is hotter and better than pussy. I stated what Marvin Gaye and Tammi Terrell say (ain't nothing like the real thing) and than I say I will pass. I saw my first Hard core X-Rated sex movies at the Gym, this was where our movies were shown at back in 1982. These X-Rated sex movies must have done a number on some of the inmate, because some of their most intimacy moment were shared and perform at these type of

20

movies. The Homo-sexual were plying their trade at these gathering, you could see inmate disappear between the bleachers these movies increased and incited rape and violent. The prison chaplain came together and pass a bill to stop showing these skin flicks in all prison. Back in 1982 M.C.T.C. Hagerstown had the Boxing matches over the Gym inmate came from the Pen. And other prison participate in this main event. We also use to get free money every month all prison was getting this free cash out except were Lifer were doing time. They said the Pen. Complaint than the state cut the whole program. As time flew on it was time for me to go in front the Reclass Board, since it was my first Adult bid, and they had this Point System they were going by it guide line. I met the criteria and points to be sent to camp. First you had to be sent to the main camp which was (B.C.F.) Brockbridge in Jessup, Maryland. Back than you could had $ 35.00 in your possession. The phone was only a dime than a Quarter, I always kept 5 roll of Quarter for a phone shot. There was no ban on Cigarettes although I didn't smoke, I kept 4 carton of cancer stick at hand. The (reclass) reclassification team at Brockbridge stated I had to go to an outlined camp, before I could be transfer into the City, they sent me to (E.P.R.U.) on the Eastern Shore. I met some of my home boys there, and I cut into this cat Mitch Curry and his sidekick Larry Dupree, all 3 of us became instant friends. I remember seeing Mitch curry at Training School although we didn't know one another, because we were in different Cottage, I used to see Mitch Curry leading the line when his Cottage were walking to the kitchen. He was always shouting 3 meals and a snack will bring a nigger right back. He was referring to Breakfast, lunch, dinner, and the 8 p.m. Peanut butter/ Jelly sandwich which was better know as a choke sandwich you needed a milk to wash that thick State peanut butter down. It was a good thing to team up with Mitch Curry at E.P.R.U. he was a master thief. We use to break into locker, and when some one were not looking we crept into your un-lock locker, we use to cut through the woods, it was a bar not to far from E.P.R.U., this is where I earned my G.E.D. at in 1983. I was on work-release, I help build the first house on Cambridge Island. They made me mad, they gave the Inmate that was resident of the Eastern Shore easy Jobs. I was an construction worker (laborer) I got fired 2 day later. That when Me, Larry Dupree, and Mitch Curry started stealing big time. One day an inmate try me, I knock him straight out. There was this tall black inmate named Samuel Keeny picking with much smaller inmate. Me and my crew didn't have no problem out of him, but this barber did one day to many Samuel Keeny push the barber, this barber truly must to had have years of training with a straight razor, because he cut Samuel Keeny across the neck, it was a big and nasty gash, some people said you could get cut by a razor and don't know you're cut. Well Samuel was bleeding profusely like a struck pig. I said put a band aid on it, every body laugh, Because they knew Samuel Keeny needed stitches, a couple hours later this inmate Shawn Anthony stated Dave you're cold, telling that man to put a band aid on, when he almost died. I was now reading books to better my knowledge. Also I started going back to school at E.P.R.U. The female teacher was cool, (Ms. Jessica Case) always treated us fair, she shown us old video she made of inmate who came and when before us. Ms. Jessica Case help me pass my G.E.D. She use her camcorder to film a play that Me, Mitch Curry, and Larry Dupree made (man it was real funny). Truly there must to had been some human "Rat" snitcher at E.P.R.U. Because the (C.O.) Correctional Officer started focusing on me, they made me an object of their desire, and their true desire was to write me an infraction/ ticket, and check me in, ship me straight back to Brockbridge or perhaps back to Hagerstown, but I was one step a head of them. Me, Mitch Curry and Larry Dupree, were breaking every rule, Law, and regulation, we were even breaking rules that wasn't even on the Infraction/ Ticket form which consist of 36 infractions. When you first enter E.P.R.U. you had to go to school if you don't have your G.E.D. or an Degree etc. and you have to complete one inside detail (for 30 days). For me first it was school and than my inside detail, which consist of me working in the kitchen (busting suds) washing dishes by hand. It was manual labor, sometime I didn't feel like getting up. You only made $1.25 a day, that another form of slavery. Just look at the statistics; every prison, jail, half-way houses, and the Penal System are fill with Blacks just what Ex- comedian Richard Pryor meant when he said " You go to court looking for Justice and you find (Just-Us)." Prison is a big business it is a multi-billions dollar industrial industry. They use 3 words to build thousand of prisons Nation Wide, they said if you build prisons (They Will Come). I realize that a brother should stay home even if you only getting 6 dollars an hour because when you come to prison and work. You only make a slug a buck, one dollar and twenty-five cent a day which is the rough Equivalent of 30 dollars a month scientifically speaking. You do 15 years in prison. Time doing 15 years on a street job. You do the math. Also a society street job the wages can go up, you could get a promotion, or you could some day own the Business, being a square have it benefit, people will said he a square, he hen-peck, or he a sucker, or he no body and he don't count, he truly one of those scare weak off brand nigger. They will say all this because a man want a 9 to 5. But when I was at E.P.R.U. I was not feeling that at all, I said to my self, I will be fair for a square, because I'm hopping on a job when I'm release from here, but little did I know that I was only fooling my self. Guess I was going through the motion that every convict goes through when they are incarcerated. You made a lot of Good Samaritan statement, like I'm never coming back, I will get a 9 to 5. I will never break another law, I'm going straight, this is my last time, this is it, I recall when I was over Baltimore City Jail has a sign that read (never again). I saw some Inmate write their name on the prison wall, I was told that mean they will be back to see their name again. I sort of got real superstitious if some body sweep my feet I spit on the broom and I told my self once I'm release I will not visit no body in prison, you go as far as joining a church or start praying. But back in 1983 I was not ready to accept GOD. I was not ready to receive, it was just no happen captain. I was pretty piss off I had to wash dishes (work in the kitchen). But I got much bigger and stronger. I got my eat-on, also I sold hot sandwich for money and (fogs) cigarette. I than was transfer in the city (B. P.R.U.). Baltimore Pre-Release Unit on Greenmount Ave. which was right next to my project (Latrobe) and my family was still living in Latrobe. I started working the (S.U.I.) State Use Industrial warehouse on Greenmount Ave. we deliver furniture. I use to slip home every day. Got caught, got an infraction/ticket for being Out Of Bound, got check into Brockbridge. When in front of the adjustment board for my hearing, I beat the ticket but they kept me down Brockbridge. I was release in 1985. When I hit the brick in 1985, as Napoleon Bonaparte describe it, "I Came, I Saw, and I Conquer." Fresh from prison, I saw the change to the new world, it was sort of scary. Even the most beautiful creature on earth were no longer the girl next door. They were conniving, scheming, dreaming, and manipulative. I was introduce to this female Janice Matthews, she was truly a dime with a remarkable skill of just good conversation, she talked down to me, sort of made me felt like my name was zero, and I was nothing more than a second class citizen, in so many word she definitely was playing me cheap, the only problem was I was not getting no drug money, therefore I was a no body to her. I mean Janice and her twin sister Annette Matthews came to Latrobe over my house. Janice acted like she paid rent and own the place, This just didn't set right with me, I decided she truly needed to be taught a valuable lesson. At this point in time 1 was 5 weeks fresh from prison with out any funds. All my dawgs stated this is a brand new Era. So my homie Drake Thomas gave me a gun and a package and he fronted me off with 1 kilo of raw this brick of boy was so good that it sold faster than the 2 quarter of shirley/girl he gave me. For one thing Baltimore is a city fill with the majority of heroin addicted, and also this particular product was better than China White. I started seeing number, and I stated I want it all or nothing. We were driving in a car listening to the radio when I heard We are the world, We are the children, by U.S.A. for Africa. Stevie Wonder, Quincey Jones, Michael Jackson and the East Coast Artists. I mean this song was play 17 time a day for month every where and Nation Wide. More or less I always had an ear for slow, soft, and oldie but goodie music. During this period Janice Matthews' twin sister Annette took an interest in me, Annette came over one hot summer day. Well I was in the house discussing business and talking with my niece Tia 's father (Troy Clark) whom was truly a big Baller and Shot caller he had Milton Ave, Lanvale, and Lafayette Ave lock down. I knew I had to have this soldier in my corner, so I was listening and hanging on to his every word. So when the door bell rang I was in no hurry to answer it, Than the door bell rang with such an intensity, sort of border on the line of urgency and desperation. But now I was in the drug game full force, and it could have been one of my dawgs, or one of my connection, so I proceeded to answer the door, I was abate and shock by whom it was and that she was solo. Even more shock when she display what she was there for. Annette Matthews stated she just wanted to sit back, chill, and kick it with me, just to get to know you a little better, you seem like cool people and good company. All I could shoot back was now that the attitude, so she came in. we when to my bedroom, we pass Troy Clark on the way in, he smile and wink. Annette Matthews started stripping and dipping before the bedroom door was close. She was a real live one, I just had to handle my business, all that stress and pressure that was build up from being lock down for 3 years and 4 months exploded in her very existence, I Guess I will never truly forget Annette Matthews, she was sort of my first, she was not truly what you could call your Girl, wife, women, not even baby mama material. But for that moment she fulfill avoid that was left by her twin sister Janice. We were going at it for the 5th time, which was 4 hours later, than all a sudden Janice Matthews came bursting through the unlocked bedroom door, Troy Clark on her heel, stating he try to stop her, at this point a fight was already ensuing between the twin, me and Troy Clark watch, laugh, and smiled. The two sisters fought for about 20 minute, one in the nude. This boast my ego for what was to come in the future. After the fight that when I first actually realized I had real power to have two sisters ready to kill one another over "little me." At that time I was fairly small even though I was seeing number, but I was truly convince all you need is money. At this point in time Andrew Mason was my right hand man, he had held down the street when he was release from Training School. He stated he was sorry that he when to Training School and I when to prison in 1982 I know we both got lock up together that day on the same charge, I told him it was the system not him. And I was truly glad he kept people on point, and he was on top of things and he held me down, he was truly in my corner, he had my back one hundred percent, and that was a good thing, because I was in a world and a game that you could not trust no one. With Andrew Mason and the other soldier help we had Latrobe lock down, and it was part of my theme, scheme, and dream, I want all or nothing, I wanted to lock down this project, because it was a logical, strategic, and geographical point. First of all Latrobe was in the heart of every thing, you had the East Baltimore Medical Center, Old Town Mall (Gay Street), Lafayette and Somerset projects, and Greenmount Ave. plus Greenmount Ave is fill with at lease 35 prison, Jail, institution. Right across the street from Latrobe Project we have the Pen, City Jail, Central Booking, a prison call Bccc, a prison called Latrobe which was build and name after "the Jet" Project Latrobe, Super Max, also we have D.O.C. House this building stirred a lot of controversies and conversation. For when it was first built, the inmate was at the big window of their cell, which faced Greenmount Ave., the inmates were naked, flashing, masturbation at these 12 by 12 picture clear window, for these window were plain and crystal clear like a house window, people were stopping traffic. Vehicles had accidents. Almost every day female were outside showing their chest and breast and writing their name, address, and phone number on the street black top. The inmate could see all this and every thing. As well as those from the outside could see them. It hurt and was pure torture to be at D.O.C. House waiting to be transfer to your designated Prison. The Afro paper had a field day about this Reclassification Center know as the doc house/D.O.C., the Afro had a big photo of the naked inmate in one of their Issue. With all the Correctional Officers, visitor, and people coming from prison looking to blow some frustration and money, this was truly a strategic point, to top it off I hit pay dirt, and it truly convince me and confirm my first observation, when the Club Volcanoes came in full swing. Greenmount and Eager street was what was happening. Volcanoes was at it peak, at full throttle. Square, pimp, Ballers, player, and playee was doing their thing, boogying, sweating, grinding, and getting funky, getting their dance and freak on at Volcanoes, I can't count the many female whom cop from me, stating the coke make them freaky, when actually they were already freak from the start, the way some of them carry on, from a train eye one could clearly see they must to have had some sort of freak in them already. But us player didn't mind, we just got our freak on. But never the less people came to and Fro Volcanoes to get their drug of choice. At this point I started to see that slinging drugs was not all peaches and cream nor all fun and game, this rival dealer by the name Mickey Spence stated he was taking over my operation by choice or force. Two days later he was found shot to death, the police, Narcs, and homicide detective ask question. Now the strip was getting hot. After Mickey Spence untimely and unfortunate death I was pondering and wondering, what could come out of all of this, now I had no Illusion, this was a dangerous and risky Business. The Narc were exercising their authority, which in turn made the (Jets) Project hotter than July, So I stopped slingin drug and to join Job Corp (Susquehanna) where the Matthews twins where at. Some time I wonder was I truly leaving the street to join Job Corp to better my living Existence, or was I merely going just to be with Annette Matthews, if the latter reason was the true reason, I must had been a true fool, first of all me and Annette departed on bad terms, and she was truly hurt, I was now a major player in the scheme of things and on top of things. But I didn't give her a fleeing thought or a backward kool (look). When you spell kool backward, it spell look. In so many words I'm saying I didn't give Annette Matthews a backward look, and I learned under no uncertain terms that a women scorn can prove to be fatal, well in this case almost fatal, in fact I saw first hand what a hurt, rejected, twisted, torn, and scorn women such as Annette Matthews could do, Because when she saw me at Job Corp she went to great length to destroy me. She was very much feeling her self Since this was a co-ed Job Corp with both male and female, she felt safe to try me with all those dude present, they must to have been wearing her out, because I did see a lot of guys in her face. Also they use to climb up to the balcony to each other room. There was a trail in the wood that lead to (Chesapeake) a connecting adjunct Job Corp both located in Port Deposit, Maryland. I try to avoid Annette Matthews and Janice Matthews, Because Janice was now acting a fool, saying little smart things. Giving me the mean mug. When in fact they were not even built like that, and that what kept me from stepping to their ghetto butt. As I stated I try to avoid the twins at all cost. I came there for an education, to escape the hood and ghetto, so I use to walk the trail to the other Job Corp with the shorty I met the first day I got off the Trailway Bus. Candice Smith was a very sexy, foxy, caramel color African princess. At the time when I first arrive at (Susquehanna) Port Deposit. I was very tire and exhausted I didn't feel like carrying those 7 big bags I was toting. When the Trailway Bus pull to the stop, I exist the bus and was greeted by this lovely African. She spoke and said hello, do you need any help with your luggage?. I know the myth and concept of society say a man suppose to be strong and carry his own weight, But all that went out the window when Candice Smith stepped to me. My only response was "yes" you could assist me with my bags. So we walked and talked, had good conversation overtime and she became a good friend of mine. I once told Candice she was sweet like candy that must be why her parent named her Candice. But something was eating at me, my heart told me the twins was out there also this I knew before I even came to Susquehanna, but in all reality I didn't think either one of the twins had enough nerve to try me, so I was cool on that part, But what I didn't know or expect was they were to try me indirectly. They had what seem to be the whole male population at Job Corp sweating them. I was a loner, all my dawgs were home getting mad papers, some were getting so much stupid money. I used to call up town to tell my dawgs to join Job Corp, But they said "no." Well at this point I was going to school, learning to drive and taking a trade. I was doing so good, my grade were remarkably high, But at night I was contemplating what was I doing there, I already had my G.E.D. from E.P.R.U. while I was incarcerated in 1983, also you only made $2,000 for the maximum 2 years you were allow to stay at Job Corp. I did feel like I was back in prison, being close in. Because we had so many rule and regulation, it only gave way to the unshakable feeling I was not truly free, because I didn't have my freedom I felt confine and trap. Also I miss my homies and of course the money. When I reflect back to the money I was getting from the drug game. $2,000 for 2 years, that equal to $1,000 a years, that was peanut and unthinkable to some body accustom to getting paid in full, seeing large number. But I settle on the fact I would have a trade, in a job marketing world, a trade is much more than just having a G.E.D; a Degree from College is needed if you didn't have a trade, Don't get me wrong, a G.E.D. is a tool to get in the door or entry level, but it is consider low on the totem board, and believe me if you have only a G.E.D. your money will be Legally short, some company, business, or firm will just start you off with the minimum wage and please don't look for no promotion, also be prepared to be the first to get lay-off, replace, or fired. Well Susquehanna offer G.E.D. and a Trade, but as I stated I already had my G.E.D. since 1983. So a trade I could definitely utilize. Some would still say I stay because of Annette Matthews, really it was a little confusing, and I couldn't understand myself, because I think even though I treated Annette badly, I sort of felt for her, I truly did, may be because she was my first female and she was with me at a very low point in my life. One would probably say I did love Annette. But I was in a deep state of denial, and at that point I would not even argue with the person. 2 weeks into Job Corp, I still have that feeling that I wanted to just sign out and go ho home. The twins were not helping the situation none. They try to antagonize me even more, one day I was in the Rec. Hall with Candice Smith, Annette Matthews stuck her head in the door, looked straight at me and said "Dave" you're a bitch. My whole body wanted to correct the wrong done unto me. Part of me wanted to beat the crap out of Annette. All the time the little African princess was watching and listening, so now Candice Smith was seizing me up, I try to reinstate the fact to her that she was sweet like candy that why her name was Candice, but to no avail, in her little mind she thought I was weak letting the twins treat me in a bad and disrespecting matter, So it was no surprise when Candice start pulling her ass, she must to had felt there was safety in number, I mean she didn't have to be so vicious and foul with her mouth, she ran off with her mouth like she had diarrhea of the mouth. Now I was being dis full time, I mean it was an understatement to just say she was coming out her face all wrong like she had license to do so. I knew shit was about to hit the fan, so I when to the Counselor office to sign out, so they gave me papers to sign, I sign them, and the Counselor told me it would take a couple weeks to leave. Also I knew with all my heart and soul I should had check the twins and Candice Smith from the get-go, you see this is how a man create his own condition. You see if I would have put the twins especially Annette Matthews in check, this would never got out of hand, but by trying to be humble and peaceful and letting the twins slide, I only created another problem. And yes my other problem was Candice, she was out of control, I guess she figure she went this far, she might as well proceed, I guess it could be argue that man create his own condition, because I truly some time think man is a victim of circumstances, I could not imagine all this happening to me when all I wanted was a Trade, and a new life. I had not done anything to provoke such action. Yes I know the twins felt spurn, but one must lick their wound, chalk it up as experience and move on, not cause World War Three, Candice Smith was having a ball at my expense, up to a point when I go to the cafeteria to eat, she pour the whole big bottle of salt in my food. She also pour salt in my cereal on seven different occasion. First of all you must know that they had 4 big container containing 4 different brand of cereal, this particular day they had my favor, 1. Lucky charm, 2. Frosted flake, 3. Captain Crunch, 4. Raisin Brand, I mixed all 4 into this large bowl that was serve unto us at Susquehanna, my stomach was growling before I could get out of line, to just say I was hungry is an understatement. Starven like Marvin would be more appropriate, when I reached the table I was preparing to eat, Candice Smith materialize out of thin air and dump 2 whole shaker of salt in my cereal. First of all I could not believe that this happen after I told her not to let that happen again. I try to fool myself, I said to myself, she must to have thought that was sugar. But part of me said salt is written right on the container, and she done pull this trick on several occasion one time to many, now she left me no other option but to step to her dizzy ass. She than shouted I told you about playing with me. So I told her let take a walk, first she hesitate, but I hug and kiss her and said it okay. So she let her guard down, had she truly known me, she would sense and seen the hug and kiss for what it really was. Sort of a hug and kiss of death. But with the arrogant and ignorant of the youth, she proceeded with me on a walk through the woods. It would be fair to say the arrogant and ignorant of the youth made her careless and sleep on me. In a young person mind if a person get out of hand, they' re suppose to be dealt with the quickness, and immediately with no question ask, just swift brutal retaliation and hardcore reprisal, I was young to at this point but I try to be fair, like I stated before I took a little after my mother. She loved, feared, worship, and praised the lord. I was straggling the fence torn between good and evil. I wanted to be good but that was not putting bread or butter on my table, certainly not in my pocket, also the world is not acceptable to GOD or his good folks, it is deem a weakness in this so called hardcore dominating Society. And I'm talking from experience, just look at this fuck up demonstration, (reflecting) on the situation going on between me and Candice Smith. I was so lost in thought I didn't notice Candice speaking to me, so I said Hum. She said where are we going?. We were now deep in the woods, it was also breakfast time, that time of the morning the woods were empty. It was no wonder we found ourselves deep in the woods with no body in them but Candice and I. Than I stop walking and look at her, she was so pretty, I didn't know whether to hit or kiss her. But I decided it was time for some hardcore at Job Corp. so I slap her 8 time straight in the face, threw her on the ground, drag her by her long hair. Pick her up hit her 3 more time and just proceed to beat her, she was hollering, yelling, and screaming. Like the old saying goes if a lone tree fall deep in the woods will any body hear it fall, my answer to that would be I guess not, one thing for sure no body heard Candice cry for help, I beat her for a good while. I talked to her while I was beating her I try to drive home to her that she need a lesson in Etiquette and Discipline. When it was all said and done she didn't look much like an African Queen no more, her hair was all dirty and twisted, make-up, mascara all smear, clothes all dirty, now she looked like the Tasmanian Devil she really was. Now she pleading with me at this point. I look at her and I didn't feel any remorse only anger, "no" I'm not an evil heartless person, but she brought it on herself, may be if I had the time to feel or find remorse or pity I would have. But I could feel only anger because I was certain that those fool ass Niggers at Susquehanna was not going to be please with me beating up on pretty little Candice Smith, I already knew this went I enter the woods with Candice. I knew this type of action would bring some sort of repercussion from the dude out at Susquehanna or from the staffs at best. So I mentally and physically prepared myself. Like before hand I knew shit was going to hit the fan, and I was not going out like no sucker. First of all I try to avoid all of this, that why 18 days before. I went to the Counselor Office to sign out. Yes I put my John hand cock on the papers they gave me a copy and stated it will take 3 weeks to leave that is went the next Trailway Bus come to Port Deposit to pick people up. Years later I found out this was a lie, they kept me there to draw money, principal, and interest, because they get a big percentage when people sign up and stay there at Job Corp / Susquehanna, they also had a contract with the bank. After I finish doing my little workout with Candice Smith, I was tire, I got work done, and was please. Because Candice declared war first, and "I had to be a soldier at war making sure she didn't battle me no more. So we walk the trail from the woods, I went my separate way, she went off crying her poor eyes out. As I was walking to my building I was approach by Ray Powell, he and 5 other guys approach me with Candice Smith on their heel, she was still crying. Ray Powell and the other five guys surrounded me, and ray told Candice to slap me, he first told her one time, my mind could not comprehend all this. But I ask myself what the fuck these people take me for, first it was Annette Matthews, than Janice Matthews, than Candice Smith, than Ray Powell and his 5 henchman. I was truly beginning to get piss off, I was brought out of this reverie by ray telling Candice Smith two more time to slap me in the face and I better not hit her back, but Candice must to have grew to respect me from the earlier demonstration, because she look at me with fear and respect as she continue to cry, but she didn't raise her hand. I said to myself this clown must be joking. As his last command for her to slap me came from his lips, I hit him twice in the face with every thing in me, than picked him up and slammed him, I was standing over top of him. But I didn't know whether to stomp, hit, or kick him, so I started beating him in the face and head with my fist. This all happen so fast that the other 5 didn't react fast enough, also topple with the thought that I didn't show fear and took their leader out with out any hesitation, the action was quickly, brutally, and viciously done. Also I was by myself. And they heard how I did Candice Smith. And the practical eye could see she was in totally distress the way she look dirty, crying, and scare to even hit

31

me with 6 niggers present, the reason I move so quickly because I knew Candice Smith probably would have found some hidden strength in number, also I was completely mad at Ray Powell whom was still on the ground shock and utterly surprise by the turn of event. At that moment I was still beating him with solid blow, I truly know if he didn't have brain damage, he at lease had a head ache that day. Now the other 5 guys try to make their play. Well a Science teacher broke it up, before any body could jump me. The Science Teacher walk us to the school building, than we were escort to our respectively housing unit. That night 15 people called out to me, I was in my room, so when I heard them, I went to my balcony, they stated that they wanted to see me. I went to bed thinking and wishing that I had my boys with me. The following day I went to school, as I enter the school building I could see some of the 15 dude standing around, so as I walked pass one of the most bold one (Kent Hunter) hit me in the mouth, he busted my lip, now that first blood was drawn and GOD forbid it was my blood, it was definitely on. I Declare War that particular day on all 15 or so of them dudes especially Kent Hunter, so when he hit me he broke into a run, and I ran after him, but he ran into the crowd, the security guard took me to the dispensary, they gave me an Ice package. I left the building, I than went into my room where I wrap a scarf around my head like Rambo in First Blood #2. I than went outside pick up 7 big stone and a pipe and crept up on them while they were standing in a crowd by the school building, I charge them and caught them off guard, some was to shock and slow to get away I beat some of them with the pipe, chase some in the school building in up these long flight of stair throwing the seven big stone hitting them in their back trying to bust their heads. I than ran from the school building. The security guard chase me with a van, caught me, brought me back to the school building, they put me in a small office inside a much bigger office, and than they close my door. 2 minute later I heart Kent Hunter voice, so I cracked my door and peek out, Kent Hunter had his back to my crack door, he didn't know or he didn't care that I was in the room only inches from him, so I said to myself this nigger than violated, he than draw blood and it is only fair that his blood be drawn in return, so I looked around the small room finding nothing, I than look into a desk where I found a thick long sharp letter opener. I took off one of my sock and wrapped it around the handle, than open the room door and snuck up on Kent Hunter, I put my hand over his mouth to keep him from screaming, I than proceed to stab him repeatedly, I try to hit his jugular vein. The more blood I saw the more I stab him. No body was paying attention, my first reaction was to keep my left hand over his mouth and drag him in the smaller room were I could have my way with him, the frame of mind I was in, I was going to kill him, he must had sort of sense this because he stomp on my instep and bit down on my left hand real hard. He was lucky it was the hand and finger that I injure in the past when my uncle Butch misguided me into half way sawing that shotgun, and when Kent Hunter bit my hand and finger the pain was much unbearable just like the night I was on the roof and fired the cracked barrel shotgun. So I drop my hand from his mouth, he than scream, holler, and cried out loud, that when all chaos broke loose, his buddies and him started running, I mean people were running every where, this way and that. I could not distinguish who was who, or were they running toward me or from me. Also I was alone so I put my back again the wall and started hitting every thing that move, I even hit two Security Guard, hit one four time these other two time with the letter opener and a couple of other people got stabbed up also. Than the Security Guards tackle me to the floor. The people stated that they wanted to press charges, what was so funny was that Kent Hunter was one of them. The Security Guard took me to a holding cell. And the State Trooper were call, when the police took me to their station. They took my mug shot and finger prints and they check my record. Judging from my raps sheet and how I carried it at (Susquehanna) Job Corp, they called me an one man army. Than I was transfer to a county jail charged with assault, battery, and 7 counts of attempt murder. Please try to understand when I said at this point I shed a tear, first of all Kent Hunter and them stepped to me first, also I was badly out- number. They drawn my blood first. Now I was the only one sitting in a County jail awaiting trial. If convicted, could be sent up the river for life. You see the injustice. Upon entering thc County jail, 1 was put in the cell with what turned out to be a very weak inmate (Leon Henry). I should had peeked the move, yes, I certainly should had known that Leon Henry was weak. I was so amaze by my recent condition and pressing situation, that I was not fully conscience of what was in my immediate surrounding environment. Leon Henry told me on the second day of my stay that he was going to divide all his commissary down the middle with me, he gave me most of the food items, soaps, and other cosmetic. I sort of took a liking to him, nothing of a homosexual nature, I don't roll like that. But we develop a cell buddy to cell buddy understanding. But actually he was just using me, this rude awaken came on commissary day. Although I was not in the cell when it was issued, because I had an Attorney visit. After the visit I enter the cell and I notice Leon in a corner, it only took me one look to see that the cell looked different (it was empty). I than stated I thought you was making commissary. Leon Henry stated I did, but big Tank took every thing. I didn't personally know Big Tank, but by reputation he was the most biggest, thickest, and meanest black inmate in the county jail. I didn't need this drama, but I had a stake in all this, half of the commissary Leon Henry brought was mine. I went up to Big Tank cell and stated I'm not going to argue with you, but you were wrong. Big Tank said nigger I'm 'biding, I told him, well I want every thing back, he said fuck you to me. At this point the whole tier got quiet, I than stated sooner or later I will come looking for the shit, as I was walking away, Big Tank said nigger you don't want no real trouble and young blood you don't know whom you're fucking with. Seven thirty that night I retrieve the two knives I had stashed I knew they would come in handy, that why I use some of Leon Henry commissary to cop them 3 day before hand. I put the 2 shank in my dip. All inmate got quiet and were watching as I walked up stair (top tier) to the big black guy cell, the cell door was open and Big Tank was sitting on the toilet straining and grunting trying hard to shit, I stepped into his cell, he saw the two handle and some of the blade protruding from my dip, he stuttered than I heard the feces drop in the toilet real easily. Big Tank must to had seen the death in my eyes because before I could pull out the knives, he stated you could get every thing back. So I confiscated the bags of commissary. Following that incident, word got out and I had no problem there afterward. When I went to Court, Kent Hunter was in a wheel-chair also he was crying. I said to myself look at this bitch, I'm going straight back to prison, But Staff, Teacher, and My Public Defender took the stand and painted a different picture. They told the Judge that it was complete terror at the hands of Kent Hunter, Ray powell, and his gang. Also they stated that I was a Honor – Roll Student, they spoke of my grades which was among the second highest in the class, they stated I was a kind and just person that didn't cause any problem at Susquehanna (Job Corp). so the Judge had only one option, and that was to let me go Scott Free. The Judge disappointed me when he stated since the 2 Security Guard were injure and you assault/battery Miss Candice Smith, I will place you on Stet for one year which is not a guilty verdict, if you stay out of trouble for 1 year, the charges will be drop and off your record, but if you do decide to get lock-up and convicted we will reinstate these charges, you are now free to go. My shining star was still shining, I was a lucky man. When I return to Baltimore City we were now living at 1105 N. Caroline Street, still in East-B-More, but a couple of block from Latrobe Project. I rang the door bell and than my sister help me with my bags and shown me my room. I enter my room and lay my clothes bags down and took a 45 minute nap, something woke me up, a voice told me to look inside my bags so I did, now I knew what I was looking for. It was a copy of the Document I sign my John-Hancock to in-reference to getting discharge from Job Corp. this was money in the bank for me. Consider the after fact I was hurt, assaulted, and lock-up. When truly all this could have been avoided if the Susquehanna (Job Corp) Counselor would have Honor my request to be discharge before all hell and chaos broke out. I truly had a lawsuit on the Grounds that I was assaulted and beat all charges against me. And that Document would have shown the date I sign to be discharge. And Susquehanna (Job Corp) kept me there just to-gather interest and principle in-reference to my stay there, therefore they were directly and indirectly responsible for the injury, pain, suffering, wrong and harm done unto me. The only reason I was going to file this lawsuit was to win some quick and easy money to invest in the drug game. I was happy with thought of this, but that happiness was short-lived because when I look into the bags, I would not believe I could not find my copy of the discharge Document. I mean I must to have look and re-look 19 time turning the clothes inside and out, for about 55 minute I search for the document but to no avail. Job Corp/ Susquehanna had cover it tail. Two day later I re-join the drug game at full force, we had the dimes Drake Thomas and I. He plug me in. Drake Thomas had the dimes he was holding down Bond and Preston, the gang and I were clocking and seeing number full time. Our leader Tony use to drive pass in his 1985 Cresssida he always brag that he pay 18,000 for this fully loaded car and because he paid full price, he was able to get a fully loaded Maxima for 5,000. Tony always had my favor tune blasting from his Ghetto speaker as he cruise by. He away had Eric B- and Rakim paid in full, blasting from his ride. He could have thrown a block party with just his car sound system, one day some niggers from Milton Ave marched down on us. Tony was in his Cressida, they open fire on the car. We than return fire backing them away from the Cressida, two guys got killed and one wounded that day. It got hot and the police put the heat on. I than went back to my hood (Latrobe) Project. One of my comrade Philip Leister that had branch off to further his interest up on Harford Road, he heard I was back on the block in the swing of things. Philip Leister came down the project and said you're still my nigger if you don't get no bigger, Philip Leister was not a strong or violent man by nature, but he had this uncanny ability to know all the latest fashion, he also was wearing that wear, I mean we all had good expensive clothing. But he had shit you never saw, heard, or let alone pronounce. Also he had Harford Road lock-down, being with him kept me on point and kept me dressing sharp. At this point there were a long list of female jocking me, I already had them running to and fro. Logical thinking was to keep Philip Leister in my corner. One day Philip Leister and I were walking, this female name Pamela Wise was coming down the street. Well Pamela Wise and me were only talking at the time, but nothing serious. So I thought she was fair game for me and Philip Leister, so 1 let him feel on her as I was feeling on her, she told both of us to stop. At this point I was to engross in my joy, for this almost felt better than sex, she than try to spit on me, I hit her 3 time in the face and pick her big ass up and slammed her in Dunbar Football Field, dust and dirt when every where, I think I heard her fart too. She got up crying and stated she was going to get her big brother, while she was walking a guy asked her what wrong baby? I ask him what the fuck he got to do with it? He said he was just joking and walk off. About 2 minute later her brother came into Dunbar field with the whole family on his heel. He was dress in camouflage army fatigue, we face off to one another, we started moving in circle, than he attacked. It was Uncle Sam vs the penitentiary. We fought for about thirty-one minute, hand to hand combat, than we grabbed one another, he was a little stronger. He had me bend toward the ground, I then reversed the position and slammed his ass to the ground and started beating him in the face, before I knew it all hell broke loose, while I was on top of him, the grand mother hit me 4 time in the head with a long plastic spoon, I got up, people from his family were every where swinging at me. I dance, duck, and dodge the blows, I was swinging and throwing my

36

own blows in return, so I was ready to leave the football field, I dance my way to the stair leading away from the field, Pamela Wise swung on me, I hit her in the face with a solid right jab, she grab her face and let out a scream of pure agony and pain. Than I left the field. The next day my cousin and Philip Leister was at Southern High School in the cafeteria with Pamela Wise she was wearing a pair of dark shade, half the school ask her to take the shade off She did, her friends, my cousin, and Philip Leister and other seen her black eye, from what I heard it was bruise, swollen, and turning color. People laugh and ask her what happen? She stated she was fighting a mad man. All I knew is, if she would have been as her name say "wise". This would never had occur. At 7pm. 3 days later I went over Philip Leister house, his oldest brother Jack answer the door. It was said Jack was made out of totally different stock than his little brother Philip Leister. Some time I wish I would have recruited Jack Leister instead of his brother Philip Leister. Jack let me in and told me Philip was in the kitchen, I enter the kitchen and set down, Philip told me he was going to pick up some Benita, quinine, and some tree. He stated his coke and heroin contact was out of the country, he than went on to tell me about Pamela Wise, I said I already know, my cousin and a few other told me, Philip than said you strap? I said yes, he said let take a ride, we drove up to Harford Road. He collected 6 Gee from his runner, than he said I might start dealing in weight, But truly I just I want to be the middle man setting up deal and meeting, I was thinking that not a bad idea for him, judging from his character he was not cut out for this business, the less he had to be on front street was the better. He shook me out of my reverie when he stated him and one of his runner was coming down Latrobe project to join me. I said which one of your runner? He said your boy Prince, I have known from the start the six month that prince worked with me down Latrobe Project before Mickey Spence was kill and the heat was put on, thus fore Prince went up on Harford Road, while I went to (Susquehanna) Job Corp. Prince had said he would be back after it cool off down Latrobe, I knew Prince enjoy slinging for me because I was reasonably fair and I did not try to work or pimp no body. Yes I knew Prince would keep his promise, so I said to Philip Leister that cool, so let go celebrate, let go to a club, How about Crecida's Continental Club, Crecida's which was located in East Baltimore Gay Street near Old Town Mall, we went down there and got our party on. This Club had a wall fill with mirror, it got so hot in there that all the mirror fogged up. We party hardy all night long than we left and departed company. The next day I was greeted with a great surprise, the dude Mitch Curry shown up at my front door. I left my old address with him and his side kick Larry Dupree before I left E.P.R.U., I said how did you find me? I said you had my old Latrobe address, he said every body know who you're, and where to find you. I hug him and let him in, he follow me to the living room I than ask when did you get home? He stated he got release 8 days ago. I said won't you have a seat, he set down than he broke off into a long conversation starting with he heard about me up E.P.R.U., also from a couple Cats from his hood Greenmount/Barclay, he said he wanted to get down, I said no problem. I went into my hiding spot and came back with 2 oz of Coke, this is $2,000 worth of Coke, and I gave him $750.00 he said thank you, good looking out. I said you don't have to thank me, I know how it is for a man fresh from prison. He said Dave I will always be in your corner, I will always remain loyal and true to you, that was music to my ears because in this business one never know what, when, where, or whom you might need. 4 day later 2 of my worker got stuck up by Big Tim. I said Big Tim got to go, first of all I was mad as hell at the 2 of my worker for slipping and sleeping. Herbert Kelly and Emanuel Adams look like two Elementary School kids as I point my finger in both of their face while I bash them with harsh words. I wanted to drive home a point literally. I finish with while you're out there slipping and sleeping, the dope jacker, heist-man, and stick — up boys are creeping. I sort of thank Eugene Chancy and Maurice Collins, these 2 workers were on point. After Big Tim robbed Herbert Kelly and Emanuel Adams, he try to hit one of my stash houses but Eugene Chancy and Maurice Collins open fire but miss him. I named Maurice Collins as my enforcer that day. 4 days later me and Mitch Curry put together and got 20 oz of Coke at $20,000 the going price was $1,000 an oz., than Andrew Mason Introduce me to this Major Player from West Baltimore Jonathan Allen, he came over East-B-More (Latrobe Project) with 5 Kilos and 4 pounds of raw Heroin and 16 Kilos bricks of Fish Scale Cocaine. I said to myself this is big, this is what happening. We started slinging and selling dime, twenty, and fifty of both Boy and Girl, I mean the Scag and Pea-funk Dope sold like hot-cake. So did the Girl. My Dope and Coke was like that. People from all four corner of Baltimore and surrounding County and people from all walk of life

38

was copping. I gave out Hundred of tester (T) when they came to buy, I use to be on the corner shouting cop and bop. But just like the junkie and user found out, so did the Dope jacker. One day Prince was suppose to be in the stash house with a saw-off double barrel shot-gun guarding the Stash house, he went outside down the block to holler at this freak She-She. As he turn to go into the stash house, a dope jacker by the name of Junie put a 44 magnum to the back of Prince head and he pistol whipped Prince and said Mother-Fucker go in, as the occupant of the house saw Prince they let down their guards, Junie came in and made off with a lot of my money and product. At the time I was in my house with Mitch Curry, Drake Thomas, Eugene Chancy, Maurice Collins, Andrew Mason, and Jonathan Allen, I was talking trash and shooting the breeze, holding Court letting every body there know this was my show. When the phone rang, I didn't answer it, little did I know it was Erica Brazil from the stash house calling to in- form me we just been hit. The door bell rang 3 time. Since I was home I answer it. Prince walk in, I couldn't believe it, Prince was actually crying when he addressed me, he told me what Junie did and how he was pistol whipped and the stash house rob, he than said between cry and tear that he was hurt and it hurt concerning how it happen. I looked at this nigger who was in front of me with tear running down his eyes and down his face. I said nigger what is your name Prince or Pussy? I than said man you better get out here, get out of my face and find that nigger and handle that. Prince stopped crying and his face lit up with joy. Judging from his action he must to have thought I was going to blame him. When he spoke up he said as much, he said I thought you were mad at me for not being on point and blame me for all this. I just looked at him. He turn on his heel and went down the step and let himself out of the front door. 3 day later Junie was found shot 2 time in back of the head. The police raid 5 of my stash houses and the whole Latrobe Strip. Now I was lucky because I was sitting in this female name Naomi Washington car, we had just pulled up. I was about to exit the Maxima when my wallet slip from my Adidas sweat-suit, it fell between the seat. Since the car was brand new I had trouble digging through the fold of the seat. That when 6 radio car pull around the bent and 12 police jump out and rounded every body up, than 8 more police car came and they went up into the 5 stash houses, the cop shut down the block, this sting netted my whole crew, I saw Jonathan Allen, Eugene Chancy, Maurice Collins,

Herbert Kelly, Emanual Adams, Prince, Erica Brazil, Mitch Curry, Andrew Mason, and Philip Leister handcuffed and being escorted by the police to the waiting cruiser and paddy wagon, I than said to Naomi Washington there goes the Neighborhood. She than drove off and drop me home. And I called my Jewish Lawyer (Jack Wissler). This Lawyer was a friend and business partner of mine. I explain everything to him, he said he would get right on top of it. My crew call me from jail. Erica Brazil ask me why I trust a Jew Lawyer, she said all they want is your money. I said Jews got money, other than Debeers and Africa; they own all the diamonds and Jewelry, when you spell the word Jewelry, you see that why they call it Jewelry. She said o.k. and hung up. Jack Wissler call 2 day later and said most of the guys got record, but the best things is they got bail. The money I made from Jonathan Allen product was in a secret "Dummy" fake bank account. I thank GOD for this West-B-More drug dealer, I knew the 5 kilos and 4 pounds of Raw Heroin and 16 Kilos "Bricks" of Fish Scale Cocaine would come in handy. All their bail together came close to the sum of 2.3 million dollars. Now I would have to work harder and also recruit some new worker, this prove not to be hard. Now I have 4 young and over zealous hopper who wanted to be part of something, also they wanted to make money. This new click consist of, well me, Douglas Vilar, Daniel Schap, Tyson Zolenas, and Danny Loughran. These Cats were pretty cool and they learned Quick, you could say they were about their work. We pull in $50,000 that week, it was on a Friday at the end of the day when I finish counting the profit Tyson Zolenas drove me home at 1105 N. Caroline ST. I told Tyson Zolenas that I'm making him my body guard and chauffeur, he said that cool and than he left. I went to my room about to go to bed when the phone rang it was Naomi Washington, she said that she was trying to reach me all day since she left her job at the supermarket, I said what going on? She said I know you stay busy, but I'm leaving the states tomorrow, I got a 2 week vacation, well I'm leaving after my shift is over at the supermarket. I want you to come on my job 12 p.m. My lunch break. I said alright and hung up. The next day I arrive at the supermarket at 11:19 am. Since I was earlier, they told me to wait. Naomi Washington was an Assistance Manager and she had her own office in the back of the supermarket. I look at my watch again, I had 40 minute to wait. I said fuck that. And I crept into the back. I was aware of the Personnel only, no trespass sign. I was walking fast I still had a little way to go before I reach Naomi Washington Office. Her supervisor came out of his office, he miss me by an inch because I duck into the butcher shop, and I notice first hand how supermarket make meat look fresh, I saw this big steel machine that spray and sprinkle fresh blood on the meats. Also I saw hundred big bag of salt. First of all most of the time when the meats reaches the store it is at lease 3 months old. And the fresh blood is dried up, so they use the machine to spray fresh blood on the meats, and they use the salt to draw the blood out of the meats, thus giving the apparent of fresh meats. I than left the butcher department and proceeded to Naomi Washington Office, she greeted me with a smile, hug, and kiss on the cheek. She was my girl for the moment. We talk in her office until 12:00. Than she drove me pass North Ave. and Greenmount as we pass the Cemetery. I pointed at the grave-yard and said people are dying to get there, she caught the joke and she smile and laugh. Than we drove to this nice Restaurant, we were about to take our seat, when Jack Leister approached me, he too was at the Restaurant, he was with his baby mother Lisa, I met her at the Leister Resident when I came to holler at Philip Leister, Lisa was real cool people, In-fact I use to date one of her female cousin that I met through her. Jack Leister greeted me, he looked worried and he sounded terrible, he than said I will be glad when my brother Philip get out on Bail. I said it already being handle as we speak, my Jew Lawyer Jack Wissler had the money, I personally made sure of that. My Lawyer stated he just waiting for the papers to be drawn up. We all know how the Bail Bond Man drags their feet. 3 days later the whole Crew was back on the block. We resume like nothing never happen. This was just a minor set back to a major come-back. Now every body was getting money. I than got every body together, and told them how excellent they were handling business. I than told them Today the Project, Tomorrow the World. These brothers didn't need any encouragement, these brothers were thorough soldier. The way things were going we could be something like multi-millionaire. We all use to talk about being our own Entrepreneur. Right now we were hungry, starven like Marvin. The thing was we were getting big headed, cocky, and some-what foolish, and that made us careless, there-fore vulnerable. One summer night it was 105 degree; Emanuel Adams, Eugene Chancy, Maurice Collins, and Prince were standing on the corner of Chase and Valley Street. When 4 dope jacker; Floyd, Hugo, Albert, and O'neal said freeze

41

you whore, empty yall pocket, don't go in your dips, keep your hands where I can see it. Than O'neal shot Prince in the chest and said that for Junie, at this distraction, Maurice Collins, Emanuel Adams, and Eugene Chancy went for the gun in their dips, this ensue a gun-battle, But because the Dope Jacker already had their guns draw it was a lopsided battle. When the smoke clear up, Emanuel Adams and Eugene Chancy lay dead, also one of the stick-up boy (Hugo) was dead. Maurice Collins drove Prince to the emergency room of Johns Hopkins Hospital. The word got to me 11:15 pm. That night. I was piss off, how could they let them Dope-fiend Junkie ass niggers do that. The funeral for Emanuel Adams and Eugene Chancy was one of the Biggest in East Baltimore History, to me they were kings "my kings". I tip a bottle of champagne to the ground and pour; in Honor of those two Cats. Prince was a live and well after 3 surgery. But he had to remain in the hospital on bed rest. I visited him every day, every body show him love, I said look get well, the whole world a-wait your arrival, he laugh and gave me a weak hand shake. While I was visiting Prince at the hospital I got a call on my pager. So I dial the number back it was Andrew Mason. He told me that this guy name Paul King II, was just release from prison. Paul King II, had lock down Latrobe Project while I was in (Susquehanna) Job Corp. he got pop 4 day before I was release from the County Jail. Now I guess he wanted the Project back. Also Daniel Schap ran off with 2 package and $60,000 of my money. I said to myself when it rain it pour, they said bad luck come in 3. First; Prince and them getting shot and rob, second; Paul King II, trying to take over Latrobe, third; Daniel Schap running off with my shit. I went down the Project the next day. Paul King II, and them was slinging in Wilmot Court. I didn't mind because at that point I needed peace not war. Also it was enough money for every body, also through Philip Leister and I had Harford Road, through Jonathan Allen and I had an 8 block radius over West Baltimore, and I had Greenmount and Barclay Street through Mitch Curry. But the word got to me that Paul King II, and his enforcer Justin was saying that Latrobe was his Baby "all His". I didn't pay that no mind, if they want trouble let them bring it. 3 weeks later on a hot summer day in August 1991 Philip Leister pull us up and told me this guy name Ralph Gary had dis him so Me, Philip Leister, Andrew mason, and Herbert Kelly took a walk, we spotted Ralph Gary on the basket-ball-court. I told Philip Leister to be a man and pick that Pepsi bottle up and bust his face, Philip Leister pick up the Pepsi Bottle from out the gutter and walk up to Ralph Gary and hit him in the face, the bottle exploded on Impact, blood went every where, Ralph Gary grab his face and let out a horrible scream. Than Ralph Gary pull out a knife and slice Andrew Mason, I grab this Little kid Louisville Slugger and I hit Ralph Gary in the face breaking his nose, than I hit him a-cross the leg and knee cap shattering it, he scream and fell to the ground. He than started to crawl, I began to beat him real hard in the head with the bat. One kid out-side playing stated "damn" he hit an home run. Ralph Gary had stop moving. But I continue to beat him with such force that the bat broke in half, I must to had hit him 49 time. His people told my father that their son was "D.O.A." Dead On Arrival. The police came around asking Question, but to no avail. Than we resume to get money. On Dec. 23,1992; Me and Jonathan Allen my West-B-More connection saw this female who told me her name was Renee Simms, we started talking and became good friend, we listen to L L Cool J: I need Love, and since it was X-MAS time, we listen to my favorite Christmas song; Some Day At Christmas Time "Stevie Wonder". The only problem was that Renee Simms was Paul King II, girl. But she told me that she didn't fuck with Paul King II, no more, he was just her Baby Daddy and Little Paul King III, was their only connection. Renee Simms told me her mother was a school teacher and her Father taught at Morgan States University. She sort of brag about how both of her parents are teacher and she also brag about how smart they were, I was fed up by her bragging, but I kept my cool and we made love 2 day later. Every time one of Paul King II, friend use to see us together, they would speak but they look at us sort of funny. On Dec. 26, 1992. I took Renee Simms and Little Paul King III, on a shopping spree, she said she wanted to catch the sale, I said baby I got money, she said don't I know. I even bought Mr. Simms some-thing because Ms. Simms didn't think I was worthy of them or their Daughter, you see this is what happen when people start making white people money and reading white people book. They had this 4 stories red brick house that cost $450,000. I sort of loved Renee Simms, she was truly a nice thick red bone with a Phat "not fat" Butt. We were spending more and more time and a lot of Quality time together. On Jan. 18, 1993. We took a 4 days trip to Benjamin "Bugsy" Siegel Land which is Las Vegas, that gangster Bugsy Siegel build a beautiful thing when he created that Vegas Strip, Bugsy

Siegel carved Las Vegas out of the dry Nevada Desert, and I know why Bugsy Siegel loved it, because it like a women it grab hold of you and suck you dry and leave you begging and crying for more. There is truly a such thing call gambling fever, addicted to gambling and Gambling habit, while Renee Simms and I was there we spend $150,000. In the 4 day we were there I show my (baby) Renee Simms a truly good time. Originally we went to the movie every Saturday so when we flew back from Nevada; the next day we went to the movies. Renee still try to get me to go to Church on Sunday, I would said no. once again I was not ready to receive Jesus as my Savior. I some time dreg going to her parent house because I could see that Ms. Simms didn't much care for me. When Ms. Simms talk to me she use big words like Phenylthiocarbamide, Hypochondriacal, Milliampere, and Vulcanization. Her daughter (Renee Simms) loved this. Renee would say Dave my mother is real smart is n't she?. I said to myself here she go with this bragging shit again. The following week her mother was sitting at the table with me and Renee, Ms. Simms said Dave do you or any-body in your Family study Zoroastrianism? I said what, Ms. Simms just smile and than got up from the table and walk up-stair to her bedroom. I said to myself I think she truly like belittling me, I turn to Renee Simms and was about to say your mother..., Renee cut me off by saying I told you my mother was Intelligent, Dave is not she smart? I said why, because she your mother or because she a teacher? Renee Simms said I believe all school teacher are real smart and intelligent, I said no not all of them are smart, Renee Simms said what ever. I said I got this Joke I heard to prove that all Teacher is not smart I said listen Renee and let me tell it, Renee said she didn't want to hear it, I said come on let me tell it, Renee Simms said okay. I said well it goes like this, there was this American Teacher Ms. Ruggs, she had a class full of American, Japanese, Jews, and Spanish Students Ms. Ruggs had 15 Questions on the bulletin board, she than said who can answer question number 1? Than she begin to read number 1 out loud. #1. Who can describe the word Pyrometallurgy? A Japanese student by the name Wong Kim raise his hand, the teacher pointed to Wong Kim and he said chemical metallurgy depending on heat action (as roasting and smelting). The teacher said excellent and than she turn to write Wong Kim answer on the board. The teacher than said who can answer number 2. Ms. Ruggs begin to read question number 2 out loud. #2. Where is Tiruchchirappalli Located? Only one hand when

44

up it was the Japanese student Wong Kim again, Ms. Ruggs pointed at Wong Kim again, he said Southern India. Ms. Ruggs said good and she turn to write Wong Kim answer on the board. She than said who can answer number 3. She than began to read question number 3. Out loud. #3. What is the meaning of the word Tracheobronchial? For the third time the Japanese was the only student to raise his hand. Ms. Ruggs pointed to Wong Kim, he said of or relating to both trachea and bronchi. Ms. Ruggs said remarkable. She pause for a minute, than she turn on the rest of the students, you all let this Japanese Student answer all the Question, he truly intelligent, I think he the best student here. She than turn to write Wong Kim answer on the board. But as she turn, some body shouted fuck the Jap. Ms. Ruggs turn around and said who said that, an American Student stood up and said General Douglas MacArthur 1941. Renee Simms burst out laughing. We than when over her house and we listen to Please Pardon me by Rufus and Chaka Khan and I only meant to wet my feet by the Whispers and You're all I need to get by and If I could Build my whole world around you, both by Marvin Gaye and Tammi Terrell, we than make love five times that night, that week we when to dinner 7 day straight, Renee Simms was now deeply in love with me, one day on Renee Simms Birthday her mother said this whom you going to marry. I said Ms. Simms you should walk a mile in my shoes before you start forming an opinion about me. I than left to go home, because I didn't need her crap. On Feb. 10, 1993 I found out that Daniel Schap was back in town. I than call my Enforcer/ hit-man Maurice Collins and told him to get on top of this. Daniel Schap call me and said he was sorry and could he have another package, 1 said yes I will hit you off tomorrow. I said let's let by- gone be by-gone. He must to thought I was on some live and let live shit, but if some body could have read my mind, although that live and let live shit came out my mouth, I was thinking this bitch ran off with my shit than have the audacity to ask me to give him another package. What the fuck do he take me for. Every body know I don't forgive or forget. Erica Brazil call me and told me she seen Daniel Schap and she said she did what I told her to do when Daniel Schap first skipped town with my product and money. I put the word out if you see, hear, or know Daniel Schap where-about, contact Maurice Collins. Every body knew Daniel Schap had ran off with my shit and they knew I would pay handsomely for this little piece of information. On July 3, 1993 I was

45

watching TV. The news reporters were talking about the summer
school budget and the 4 of July. Than they stated the parents of
Daniel Schap, Ms. Schap and his Step Father was making an stress-
ful and emotional appeals on National Television for the safe return
of their son. Than the TV Spokes-man said he was last seen on June
29. 1993 getting into a black model car with two men. Then the parent got on TV. With crying eyes, emotional choked voices and said
please return him safe. I turn the TV. Off. On Jan 5.1994 we were
getting money, paid in full. I call my connection and order 245 Kilos
of Cocaine, Crack cocaine, and Heroin. I had the Project locked
down. I than got my shorty (Renee Simms) and Little Paul King III,
we when to a movie than I took both of them shopping. We made
love 11 time when we got home. We play an old CD "Your Love"
by Grand Central Station, and Stone in love with you by The
Stylistics, while we made love. This loving have been good since day
one in 1992, this was now 1994. We made love every day at lease 3
time a day, it was no wonder she told me she was pregnant, I said I'm
the man, the father, the king. She stated she was 3 weeks, I knew she
was pregnant before she even told me, the way she acted and her
stomach had a little strange feeling, she also told me she really love
me and she said let get Married, I said cool, but let wait, so we just
chilled, we were kicking it full force, big time, I was madly in love, I
mean we were going every where together, it was nothing to spend
$7,500 on Little Paul King III, and Renee Simms at a shopping trip.
I bought Renee Simms a $60,000 truck. We didn't live together
because I need my space, also because of the kind of business I was
into. I told her to quit her job, she said no. she also gave me a couple of Job Application, I fill them out just to keep her Quiet. At this
point Maurice Collins started going to school and taking up a trade,
Physic, Science, Electronic, and Chemistry. Maurice Collins stated
he needed a front, but he will always be loyal to me. Then on June
20, 1994 Paul King II, called and started threatening Renee Simms
when she answer the phone, I saw the look of distress on Renee
Simms face, so I grab the phone and I said what up? He said bitch I
don't want to talk to you. I said look man watch your mouth. He said
all fuck you. I wanted to tell Paul King II, with that kind of talk he
was going to find him-self on the business end of my pistol. He than
said you're trying to take my girl, it is bad enough you're dealing
drugs on my Turf. I said I love her and I do for Little Paul. I got
nothing but love for the little fellow. He than said I don't want to see

you holding or beating my son. I said na I don't get down like that. He than said alright bitch. I said the reason I'm respecting and talking to you is on the strength of Renee Simms. He said oh yeah I heard you sold all 245 Kilos of that Coke, Crack, and Heroin and than he said see if you live to spend the money, Paul King II, than hung up. 3 days later I sent Paul king II, a message his Lieutenant was gun down along with 2 of his worker. Paul struck back, I was walking by Old Town Mall "Gay Street" when a car drove by firing bullets at me, I duck behind two park car, me and Maurice Collins return fire, the next day I struck back fiercely, Paul King II, Enforcer Justin was found slain in his car. Paul answer that by the killing of one of my top associate, this battle wages on with both side taking and giving ground. I went to Renee Simms house, I carry my niece Tia which is the oldest of two girls, my favor sister Teresa Stokes and drug dealer Troy Clark daughter, Troy Clark was in prison he got 2 years for a handgun charge. So now I was taking care of Tia. My sister was a Doctor, and she didn't take what she call blood money. So I just help and supported Tia Clark. But she was not my favorite, her baby sister was (Tina). Now don't get me wrong, my favorite sister (Teresa Stokes) only have these 2 girls, and I should not had pick one over the other, but Tina was the first one beside Renee Simms to call me King Dave, yes they were the only 2 people in the world to call me King David - King Dave. Tina would always greet me with a hug and Uncle Dave you're my King, Tina never really call me Uncle Dave, just king Dave. When Renee Simms or Tina see me on the street or any where, they shout hey King Dave. I also took care of Little Paul King III. Renee Simms and I took Good care of Tina because her father was an Officer. (A Navy Seal). he was station in Iraq, I always joke with Hector who was Tina father, Hector was real cool, one day I ask him What did the soldier of Iraq do when the United States Army Invaded? Hector said I don't know, I said I-ran, he laugh and said that a good joke about the 2 Arab Country. Now that Hector was over sea. I looked out for my niece Tina. Me and Renee Simms took Tia home, and on the way I stopped and got Tina a Puppy for her birthday. I drop Renee Simms, Tia, and the Puppy off. I than wave my hand my chauffeur Tyson Zolenas and my enforcer/hit-man Maurice Collins pulled up, we than went to a party. As we were driving to the Club, people were honking their car horn and waving as we push the Black Mercedes- Benz- 190 through the street. It was the summer time we had the sun roof down, play-

47

er, dealer, big ballers and female of all age, size, and colors were waving, they knew it was my Black Mercedes Benz 190. Cruising down the street. We shown much love by waving back, I guess they were wrong when they stated the street don't love no body, because every time I go in the street, movie, Club, Show or the Shopping malls, people always waving, tooting their car horn, hugging, or shaking my hand, showing some sort of love. No matter if I was over East, South, North, or West Baltimore there were some body who knew or heard about us, or knew or heard about me. I was a real Ghetto Super Star. As the black Benz pull up to the curb. At lease 125 female and niggers were standing in a long line to get in Volcanoes, my chauffeur Tyson Zolenas open the car door and we spotted Big Dennis and Pig they were the two bouncer at the door. Both of them were cool with us, so went straight to the front of the line, shaking hands, giving and getting high five, and getting hugs out of female and male alike. At lease 50 people or more spoke and show love, and we did the same likewise. All you could hear was what up Dave? What up Maurice Collins? What happening Tyson Zolenas? Some of these people was seeing large number, some were truly getting paid in full and they were feeling us, as much as we were feeling them. A few people that seem me in my leather coats, especially when I wore a black Leather every body said I look like Run-DMC; they would joke and say what up Run?. The bouncers didn't frisk us, they just let us in, all 3 of us was strap. As I got in the door a female name Pebble ran up and hug me. All 3 of us received the same love inside, that we just received outside. This drug dealer name Wilcox said you know your boy Freddy from Cherry Hill, he just got a new Lexus, I said I know I saw him 5 day ago. A female name Freda said this is the Volcanoes, get your freak on. 2 more guys came up and shook our hand, one of them said Fuzi from Bond and Preston ask about you, he told me if I run into you, to tell you to holler at a nigger. I said O.K., than little Moe came up and gave me a hug and said you know my connection got kill in New York, I said na., than I was greeted by 7 female, 4 of them I fucked already. Those 4 took Photo with me at the Club. Maurice Collins and Tyson Zolenas took some flick with some female they knew. Than we all got on the dance floor. Maurice Collins was on the dance floor with his hands all over this pretty red bone named Michelle Baker, as I approach he said Dave I want you to meet Michelle, she said I already know Dave. Michelle than said hey Dave what up? I said nothing but the struggle. She smile and spoke up and said all those rocks and Bling/ Bling you 're rocking don't seem to me you're struggling. At that point my cell phone vibrated and I pick up and said hello. It was my sister Teresa stokes, she said Mom was in the Hospital for high blood pressure, Teresa said she just drove Mom to Johns Hopkins Hospital 11 minute ago. I said I'm on my way. So I found Tyson Zolenas and we left the club. We were walking to the car, when we reached the Benz Tyson Zolenas held the car door open for me, I was Ready to get in the car, that when I spotted this pretty brown skin Chick. She was walking up Greenmount Ave., when she got up to where the Benz was park, I said Hey Miss Lady, she said Hi, I than said what up? What your name? She said Vivian McDermott. I said my name Dave. I said where are you heading? She said Bond –n-Preston. I said I be up on Bond and Preston all the time with Drake Thomas and Them. She said I know them niggers. I said why I never ran across you? She said it because I live out Woodlawn, but my people live on Bond and Preston. I said who your people? She said the Brown Family, Keisha, Willie, Marvin Brown, I said I know them. We than exchange name and numbers, I said you be careful out here, than I turn around to the Benz and Tyson Zolenas held the door open and I got in the car and we speed up to see Mom. As time flew on we were selling Fifty down the Project. On July 12, 1994 Danny Loughran, Me, Erica Brazil, and Tyson Zolenas was coming out of Volcanoes, a guy and a girl was pushing a baby carriage up Greenmount Ave., as they approach I could not help but stare, for the simple reason I do have a baby on the way, also that was a handsome young couple that seen madly in love, I could not help wondering if me and Renee Simms look like that, all the sudden the couple pull the baby blanket back and than the couple lift up their guns from the carriage, the man held a 357 magnum and the lady had an Uzi. They open fire on us: Danny Loughran was hit in the head, he was dead before he hit the ground, dead on his feet. Erica Brazil push me down on the ground and she came out with her weapon at the same time Erica Brazil was cut in half by the Uzi. As I was falling to the ground a slug went pass my face the bullet glaze my forehead. From the ground position I Immediately came out with my gun and I got off 4 shot, me and Tyson Zolenas shot at their fleeing back, but we miss, I than got up and when over to Erica Brazil and I just held her dead body with tears in my eyes and larceny and malice in my heart, than I cry for her, myself, and all the lost comrade in this fuck up drug-game. There were siren in the back-ground, also people where now forming a crowd. A lot of party go-er from Volcanoes was out there also people from Latrobe Project was peek-ing at the scene. I felt a tap on my back it was Tyson Zolenas, he said Dave we got to move, the Cops are coming. I was just sitting there crying un-controllably. Tyson Zolenas than said I'm your Chauffeur and body guard: I'm responsible to make sure you get home safe. For some odd reason I did not move and I did not put Erica Brazil dead body down. I was cover with Erica Brazil blood. Than after Tyson Zolenas could not budge me, he than collected Erica Brazil and Danny Loughran gun. He than said Dave pass me your gun, I gave it to him and he said damn Dave I got to run. He than got in the black Benz and put petal to the metal as he peel off The first 5 police car came. The police got out their cars with gun drawn, I guess they didn't know what to make out of all this; 2 dead bodies and shell casing all over the ground and a young black male (me) holding one of the body, before I could say any thing the Bouncer Big Dennis said I saw every thing, he than gave them a song and dance that was far from the truth. The cops checked me out, they saw the little mark where the bullet glazed my fore-head, they said what your name? I said David Stokes they than ask do you got any I.D.? I gave them my wallet, the address was 1105 N. Caroline Street. The cop said we must take you to the Central District Police Station for Questioning. So they drove me there. When I got there, I gave a written statement that I didn't do nothing wrong. And it happen so fast that I didn't get a good look at the shooters face, I could tell by the tone of their voices and the expression on their faces that they knew I was lying, I than said let me call Mr. Jack Wissler; he my Lawyer, at the mention of Mr. Jack Wissler name, the police and 2 homicide Detective acted strange and scare. And I could tell they were scare, they try to hide their fear by talking loud to me. For it was common knowledge that this Jewish Lawyer since he came to Maryland than got 43 police fired this included Captain, LT, SGT., Regular Patrol Officers, and 4 Homicide Detective, and this Jew Lawyer was now in court with a case against 3 FEDS for misconduct, harassment, and Perjury, he also won 17 Lawsuit against the States, City, and Government that cost them an estimate of $12,749,000., than one of the Homicide Detective said you're that David Stokes (Dave) from Latrobe Project, he than said I could not make that connection because your I.D. and wallet carry 1105

N. Caroline Street address in it. Than the 2 Homicide Detective say there are lease 22 David Stokes in the Computer, but when you mention your Lawyer is Jack Wissler, and considering where this Double Homicide took place tonight, I put 2 and 2 together, I now know we are dealing with a Major Player. We know every thing you did and done down Latrobe Project, We also know about that little war you and Paul King II,. Got going on. I said you don't know shit, if you had or have any hard evident, you would have lock me up. The Detective Miller stated if people up, then he stop and cough and he looked at me funny and than he continue, if people up Hagerstown know what going on and that up in the mountain, don't you think the police next door know what going on? I looked at this white police and ponder in my mind. I said to myself this made sense. Because went I was in Prison up Hagerstown which is in the mountain, all us convict and inmate talk about was what was going on in Baltimore City, who fucking who, who got Aids, who got married, who got kill, who getting money in the City. Officer Spry, Lefer, and Legel left the room it was time for shift to change. Officer Miller than said in-fact I have known about this war between you and Paul King II, since it begun, But we ain't trying to stop it. We will let one side kill the other. And we will pick up the pieces, than Officer Miller said I hate all Niggers yall are so dumb, sell drugs, steal, fight, kill, rob, and hate each other, and think the white care, help, and respect you all. I then said thank you that mighty whitey of you. He raised his hand as if to strike me, but the door open. In came an officer, judging from the stripe on his uniform he was a Major. The Major stated are you going to Book David Stokes. Officer Miller said no. The major said than let him go. I also notice that none of these Officers introduce their self. I learned their name and stripe from their badge, shirt and uniform. So they let me go. I than called my chauffeur/ body guard Tyson Zolenas and he pick me up from the police station on Fayette Street. As we drove through the City, I said and Baltimore suppose to be Charm City, to me it more like Harm city. Than we drove to West Baltimore. What most didn't know I was now living at 523 West Bloom Street. The police had look at my old I.D. with the address 1105 N. Caroline Street., Bloom Street was fine with me, I didn't want to live to big, also I wanted a home in the Hood where I could have traffic coming and going. That night I went to bed I was tossing and turning waking up crying, I was mad that this thought kept coming to my mind and I said to myself it is funny how life is my Boo (Renee Simms) and my favorite niece Tina think I'm King Dave. And the way Paul treating me like I'm Queen Dave. I guess Paul must think he is a king because his last name said so Paul King II. I went back to sleep and woke up Saturday morning at 8:35 am. I went down stair and cut on TV. I put on an old Tom –n- Jerry cartoon I was laughing my head off. At 8:45 am. I got up and got milk and cookies from the refrigerator, and then I resumed to watch Tom and Jerry. A minute later the door bell rang, I open it, my uncle Butch walk in with this guy who looked sort of familiar, this guy was dirty, funky, and he had a very foul B.O., yes his body odor was oppressing and repression, this also made me laugh, I was thinking no he didn't. I can't believe what kind of company my Uncle Butch was keeping. And my uncle Butch got the nerve to bring this garbage to my house, all I could do was bust out laughing. My Uncle Butch looked at the TV. Than he looked at me and said you're no good watching cartoon, laughing, eating cookies and milk like a child. I was already piss off about what he brought in my house, and when he made that statement about me being a child, I was tick off to no end. I said dummy, cartoon in the United States was really invented for adult during the 1915 World War to take people mind off all the killing, suicide, war, and Great Depression. Than the bum my uncle was with extended his hand and said I'm George Jackson from Milton Ave. I didn't shake his hand, but an Alarm went off in my head, because I now knew why he looked familiar. He was once one of Paul King II, Top LT. Before I could open my mouth, my uncle Butch said "na" "na" it not like that, just hear George Jackson out. I than said to George Jackson what up? George Jackson said as you know I was one of Paul King II. Top Lieutenant but I started to use the product. One time I ran off with $426,000. Well Paul King II, Had me beat down and he told me that I will have to use, smoke, shoot, or snort his product before he put it on the street. Well about 2 years ago: Paul King II, Flew to Turkey and got some cheap brand of Heroin, he had me shoot it up, it when straight to my head it was a bad batch, I started pulling all my clothes off, foaming out the mouth, I ran outside naked and started eating grass and dog shit out of some body yard. Neighbor than call the police, they sent me to Spring Grove Hospital. I'm now on 15 different psychotic medicines. I got a weak heart and I can't see out my right eye. To top it off when I was discharge from the Mental Institution, Paul King II,. Told me I still owe him $272,000.

And there fore must still work for him. This month I did 7 testes for him and I ended up in the Emergency room at Johns Hopkins Hospital, the doctor told me I can't keep putting strain on my heart, also the doctor told me I can't keep on mixing Illegal drugs with my psychotic medications. It will take me years to pay his money back and with my condition and health I will not last 3 more weeks working for Paul King II,. Also something tell me he never planning to cut me loose, Paul King II,. Never forget or forgive. Also I heard about the shooting on Greenmount Ave., You know Erica Brazil was a cool person, she gave me money on several occasion, although she was in the game, she was fair, she never gave me drugs, she would say here take this money, buy some new clothes, get a hair cut, shave, get some soap, also get yourself some thing to eat. I once ask her why?. I said Erica Brazil you're in the life, Girl you in the drug game. Why do you look out for me?. Erica Brazil said George Jackson I remember when you were driving expensive cars and trucks. You had a female on your arm at lease 4 time a week. I remember how you use to look, how you use to be. George Jackson than said to me I was touch, that was some heavy and deep shit. Now she dead. Than George Jackson said I got a plan to get rid of Paul King II,. Once and for all. George Jackson said well he expecting an shipment 30 Kilos of raw Heroin tonight. The address is 1012 Abbott Court. At 9:00 pm. I will leave the front door un- lock. I said cool, he thank my uncle Butch and shook both of our hand and than let himself out. I than turn to my uncle Butch and said that one George Jackson that not part of the solution, not part of the revolution, but part of air pollution. My uncle Butch laugh until tears came from his eyes, he said damn Dave you're funny. I than wash my hands and pick up the phone to make 2 phone call first I call my Boo (Renee Simms). Her line was busy, than I hung up my phone to call her cell phone. But than my phone rang it was Renee Simms. She said I was trying to reach you. She than said I was calling to tell you me and little Paul is going to the night Clinic at G. B.M.C. since I work in the day time, we got a 8:30 pm. Appointment at night. I was thinking to myself perfect timing, for one thing she always kept her son appointment, and if Paul King II,. Stop over her house she would be gone. There fore Paul king II,. Would probably be in the Stash house. I was lost in thought, I almost forgot that my boo was on the phone until she said Dave, than me and Renee Simms talk about our future together, we talk about a name for the baby. She said she would name a girl, if it is a boy I would name the boy. We talk about how much we love and miss one another and finally we talk about marriage. And than I thought about tonight and George Jackson. So I joked with Renee Simms and said I'm not going to Shit, Shave, nor Bathe until you get home. She laugh and said O.K., than we both said I love you Boo. And than we hung up. I than call Maurice Collins told him to gather the Crew and about the 9:00 pm. Meeting. After I hung up I than turn my attention to my Uncle Butch. He than said those cookies look stale, than he look at the Raghie bag it had 2 for a dollar on it, my Uncle Butch stated all that money you 're getting. you 're cheap. I said keep playing with me and I'm going to jump right straight in your ass with both feet and no grease, my uncle Butch started laughing again than he left my house. That night at 9:00 pm. Me, Maurice Collins, Douglas Vilar, Mitch Curry, Andrew Mason and West Baltimore Jonathan Allen took our guns out and enter the un-lock Dwelling of Paul King II,. He was in there with little Keith Mackey and George Jackson. As we search Paul King II. And little Keith Mackey. Maurice Collins went up-stair, moment later I heard two loud pop, sound of a gun being fired and than Maurice Collins came back down stair. I than proceed to put Paul King II. And little Keith Mackey on their knee and stood behind them and shot both of them once in the back of their head. George Jackson than said what about me? I than shot him once in the face. My logic was how could you trust a man who turn on his Boss. The next day was when the shit hit the fan, the 12 O'clock News came on it stated that Renee Simms when to retrieve her son from his father, and rang the door bell, and just happen to turn the door knob and found Paul King II,. George Jackson, Keith Mackey dead down stair and her son Paul King III,. Dead up stair. I felt a wave of pain, shock, disbelief, and hurt go through me and a tear row down my eye. I tried to blame Renee Simms for this because she stated she was going to G.B.M.C. with little Paul King III,. But then I look over at Maurice Collins whom was sitting at my table watching TV. I said why the Baby? Maurice Collins said he might had recognize me and all of us. Also I believe like the Mafia and Sicilian that the son could grow up and come after us, Maurice Collins than said that vendetta shit is real, I just said O.K., but I was not feeling that shit. Than I went back to look at the News, they stated Renee Simms is heavy sedative and under observation at the hospital. 5 day later Renee Simms call me and ask why? why?, why?, we kill her baby. She said she knew she should had kept that Doctor Appointment, But yet in stead she had to go to her parents house and she let Paul King II. Keep their son, and she spent the night over her parents house, also she said she lost our baby that was in her stomach because of the stress and she said everything gone that she believe in, and GOD why? She than said she hate every thing I do. She said all I do is sell drugs and kill people, and than she hung up, I call her back and we argue for about an hour, I got out my tape cassette player and I play, we come much to far to end now, by Smokey Robinson, and we both cried, but she said it over. My man Sonny who was now working for me full time came over my house and said Dave be strong, than he left. I waited a month before I called the female I met on Greenmount Ave. near the Club Volcanoes. The female Vivian McDermott from Woodlawn, she was real thrill to hear from me. She was really a truly beautiful and sweet person. One day we stop at a corner store, she stated just get me a bottle of Pepsi (soda). Than we went to my Crib, she said take your clothes off and take that cap off, she than ask do you always wear a cap? I said yes it my Trade mark. After I took my clothes and my cap off, she took my penis in her mouth, after 11 minute of fellatio, I ejaculated in her mouth, she swallow every drop of semen, she than drunk the whole bottle of Pepsi straight down with out stopping, I was puzzle. The next day I asked a lot of my home boys they stated you got a Pro. Some body else stated you got a vet. But Herbert Kelly stated a female told him they do it to keep their face and skin clear that way they won't get bump on their face. But to me she was a real freak and I treated her bad. I start seeing and dating other female. And I kept accusing her of still messing with her baby daddy although I didn't have any concrete evident or no solid proof, I still said to her, Bitch you're cheating. One day Vivian McDermott ask me for $100,000 for her and her son and also so she can get a Truck. I said you worked before why you don't have a truck. she said when she use to be a part-time MTA bus driver she use to get on all the buses free, there fore she didn't need a car., than Vivian said MTA was not really paying any good money, now I'm broke. I said bitch you got to have some money left, MTA is ATM spell backward. Vivian said no Dave I don't have no money. We went up stair and I gave her the money and we made love 7 times that night. 2 week later she told me that she saw me with another female and her people also told her I had other female. than one night she came home and said she seem me on several occasion with different women. To make our relationship work we listen to oldie but goodie: I belong to you (Love Unlimited), On the radio (Donna Summer), You've been my inspiration (The main ingredient). Mr. Big Stuff (Jean Knight), Don't make me over (Sybil), You're the best thing that ever happen to me (Gladys Knight and the Pips). when we play this song we both sing along and said if any one should write our life story it will tell of the pain and glory. But one time Vivian play the song (Make her the women you come home to) Gladys Knight and the Pips, 17 time a day. One day I try some thing new that I learn from Maryland Training School days, I brought the Bee Gees tape (Love so right), (I just want to be your every thing), (You stepped into my life) and (Love you inside out). But no matter how we tried, we could not save our relationship. I kept telling myself she don't really love me, she probably still in love with her baby daddy, all she want is my money. After 11 months of sex and me spending money on her. I told Vivian look bitch won't you do something with your life. I told Vivian I need a strong black women like Oprah Winfrey, I said Oprah Winfrey do good thing and help people, I said Oprah Winfrey have a book Club, she read books and put people book and books in her Books Club. She give to the Community, she sent things to Africa and other Nation and Country, she brought 200-300 or more people cars, trucks, houses, and get people jobs and she pay people bills, rent, etc. I than told Vivian McDermott, bitch all you do is lay around and fuck and suck to make a buck. I told her she give the black female a bad name. After weeks of this verbal bashing she said she could not take it no more. And she warn me that ain't nothing good going to come to you until you do right by me, I said fuck you. 3 days later she walk out of my life. I was so sad I play my Oldie but Goodie. How could I let You get away (The Spinner), Bring back the love of yesterday (The Dells), I wish it would rain, Please return your love to me, All I need is to hear you say you forgive me (The Temptations). The love I never had (Tavares). But I play (Special Delivery) I Destroy your love (part 1 and part 2). At lease 50 times a day. The next few weeks Me, Douglas Vilar, Sonny, Mitch Curry, Philip Leister and his brother Jack Leister was selling drugs on Milton Ave., Latrobe Project, and Harford Road, Prince and Maurice Collins was on a mission they wanted to expand out in the County but this big time white drug dealer named Chief Whitey was in the way. Prince came back and stated that Maurice Collins is an animal, he kill Chief Whitey, his wife, and shot all 3 of his infant son in the head they were no more than 2 years old a piece, I just shook my head. The next day I receive 75 Kilos of Cocaine and 2 Kilos of raw Heroin I put this down Latrobe. A guy name Larry Lamont try to move in on our Turf. He open fire on two of my worker, 5 day later he was found shot to death. Business resume as normal. I than heard where dope jacker Floyd and O'neal were staying. I than went to Maurice Collins house he was not home but I talk to his 2 brother, Victor and Tyrone Collins they told me Maurice was in school, so I left word for him to contact me, 2 hour later he call me. I than inform Maurice Collins where he could find Floyd and O'neal, I than sent Maurice Collins, Douglas Vilar, Mitch Curry, Andrew Mason, and Jonathan Allen to their West B-More address. When they arrive stick-up boy Albert was there also, matter of fact according to Andrew Mason, Albert was the one to let them in thinking it was a female name Alicia bringing in a connection. Well when Alicia heard I was looking for them for the killing of Emanuel Adams and Eugene Chancy. She had said she would set them up for a price. When Andrew Mason got back to me, he said the 3 stick up boy were glad to see Alicia, when she knock on the door and said her name they open the door Quickly none of the 3 had gun out, they were completely caught off guard, Andrew Mason said we shot all 3 of them twice behind the ear. 2 day later my door bell rang, I answer it and it was my Uncle Butch I let him in, he said to day is my birthday I just turn 49. I said well won't you turn 69 and go find a woman. Uncle Butch said do you have a gift for me? I said yeah happy birth day. Uncle Butch said I told you that you were cheap. But Dave seriously I just turn 49 years old. I said what the fuck that suppose to mean, just because you are 49, you probably still believe in Santa Claus. Uncle Butch said what ever, any way Dave I saw your mother, she must be eating or worrying a lot, because she than got all fat. I said Uncle Butch don't talk about your sister like that. Than I said Uncle Butch I heard your mother went to the Pacific Ocean and bit a submarine in half and suck all the sea-men out. Uncle Butch said all right Dave, I didn't say nothing bad or nasty about your mother. I laugh and said Uncle Butch I said she suck all the sea-men out, not (semen). I than gave my uncle Butch $5,000 for his birthday. He said thank and left. Than one particular day Eric Rowe came to me and ask me to plug him in, I said no. truly I never respected him because he prey on old people, I remember he snatch that old lady pocket-book and got me in trouble when we were young. Also he beat that old white lady half to death and stole her pocket-book back in the days. After I said "no". Eric Rowe walk away. 3 day later Eric Rowe and Big Tim stuck up Douglas Vilar, Andrew Mason, Philip Leister and Jack Leister. This lead into a string of robbery against my Organization, another day they stuck up Douglas Vilar and shot him in the arm and chest. I then found out where Big Tim was staying. I than sent Maurice Collins, Andrew Mason, and Jonathan Allen on a mission. Big Tim grandmother open the door, Maurice Collins and them step in the house and kill his grandmother and his grandfather and than shot Big Tim in the head while he slept. When Andrew Mason got back to my place, he said Maurice Collins didn't have to kill those old people, they were at lease 80 years old and they could not even really hear or see. Than I got the word that Eric Rowe had rob two more of my runner. The word on the street was that Eric Rowe stay with his Girl friend and her parents. So Maurice Collins, Mitch Curry, and Herbert Kelly watched the house, they spotted his girl and crept up behind her as she went in the house. But Eric Rowe was not there, so Maurice Collins kill the girl, her mother, her father, and her great grand-mother, and her great grandfather, and he kill both of Eric Rowe children. Herbert Kelly was visibly shook as he told me all of this. Herbert Kelly stated (Dave) I mean I kill many men in my life time. But Maurice Collins is a monster, he truly an animal. Two day later on the news they announce they had found the remain of Daniel Schap at Leakin Park, a dog dug up the bones. He had his I.D. on him and his dental records shown that it was in-fact Daniel Schap, it appear that he was shot twice in the back of the head. I cut the TV. Off. I went to see Douglas Vilar at the Hospital. This guy came into the hospital with his eye hanging out, he was cursing up a storm, than he said to no one in particular can they put it back in, I was thinking to myself he was wishing for a miracle without GOD. Any way Douglas Vilar was doing fair so I left. Than Me and some of the crew went to see Philip and Jack Leister they both seem happy. I got real serious and said Philip you don't really love your brother. Philip said I truly love my brother and I always will, and what are you talking about Dave? I said I bet if you was on an airplane you would not greet your brother, Philip said Dave no matter where I'm at I will always greet my brother. I said let me hear you say Hi-Jack on an airplane. Philip, Jack, Andrew Mason, Drake Thomas and Fuzi all

laugh. As day went on Eric Rowe rob three more of my stash houses. I told Maurice Collins to find him as quick as possible. But we
could not find him any where. 9 days later the news on TV. And
words on the street stated that Eric Rowe was found dead on the toilet with a (spike) needle in his arm, I said well I guess shit goes where
shit goes. I went to the Hospital to see if Douglas Vilar heard the
news. He said no, he was not watching TV. Because he have a
headache. I said back in the old day they would drill, screw, and put
a hole in your head to release evil spirit, because they believe headache were just evil spirit. That day when I got home Pop came over,
he said he got lock-up for a drunk driving charge. He said Dave, the
Homicide Detectives shown him (photo) and pictures of people I
kill, he said they shown him, baby, old people, women and men. And
he said the Detective also stated they are going to get you sooner or
later. Now at this point my little brother wanted to join my
Organization, Luther Stokes and his right hand man which was this
ugly dark skin dude name Omar Roberts they wanted to be my hit-
men. It seem as a good thing, because Maurice Collins took over
Latrobe Project he also took up electronic, chemistry, physic, and
Science, and he now had a part-time job to front for some of that
drug money he was bringing in. so I said yes! To Luther Stokes and
Omar Roberts you two could be my hit-men. Than 3 weeks later I
was about to go in the house, when two police cars spotted me and
they stopped and jump out of the cars and said halt and freeze
David Stokes you're under arrest, but because I was dirty I ran, I
had to get rid of the drugs and handgun I had on me. But as I ran
I drop 1 gram and 2 oz. of raw Heroin on the ground. As I looked
over my shoulder I seen a cop pick up the drugs, than I ran into an
alley up to a dumpster and put the rest of the drugs, the gun and
extra bullet in the funky dumpster. When the cops finally caught
up to me, they search me and they only found one bullet on me. I
was piss off I thought I got rid of every thing except what they
found on the ground. They than took me to the police station. And
they had me in an office for 3 hours and than they spoke about the
bullet they found on me. They said these are special bullet, Hollow
point, Dum-Dum, Armor piercing steel jacket bullet that will
expand and explode on contact. These bullets go through our bullet proof vest. Those sort of bullet are called cops killer. The police
said we trace the bullet found on you to a gun shop that file a theft
report 3 weeks ago, the owner stated he was in the back on the

phone, when he forgot he left the gun and bullets on the display case, went he return both the gun and box of cartridge was gone there fore we are charging you with theft along with possession of a dangerous substance and the intent to distribute and distribution of narcotic, and 2 homicide. A Homicide Detective talk to me and he stated we also have you for the execution style slaying of Paul King II, and Keith Mackey. They than shown me photo of some murder victim including baby, children, old people, men and women. And they stated we know you're responsible. And you might as well confess. Because we got a star key witness, and as 1 listen I knew that there was a traitor in my organization. They put me back in the holding cell. So I put out an reward and I contact all my resources, I had a few police on my payroll. The word got back to me that Mitch Curry had a secret life, he was killing old people for insurance money and got caught and then he turn state. I said to myself this must be true, I recall when Erica Brazil and Danny Loughran were killed and the Detective Miller slip up and said if an inmate up then he look at me funny and than said Hagerstown, that thrown me off because I met Mitch curry at Eastern Shore Pre-release unit. (E.P.R.U.). I said to myself Mitch Curry name should had been Mitch The bitch Who snitch Curry. I was transfer to Central Booking. I took one look at the place and say it real name should had been (Simple Booking) because it a big joke, Inmate sleeping in boat, on the floor. Inmate being held 3 months before seeing a commissioner or getting a bail hearing, every day the police bring in 75 or more people and most of them are release on some sort of technicality, any way Steve Richards was over there he show me his charge papers, the Document read he had broke into his ex-boy friend house kill his ex-boyfriend, his ex-boyfriend wife and her 7 children by slitting their throat and than setting the house ablaze. I tried to avoid Steve Richards as much as possible. Because how he carried up Hickey School, also I could not condone his action concerning killing 7 children. But I had so much on my mind that I didn't check him when he kept coming to my cell. One particular day he said Dave we use to do a lot of things together Me, You, and Charles Nelson, But I got to confess something Steve Richards than said when I use to look at you funny and always watch you, it was not that I was mad, envy, jealous, or trying you. It was that I was in love with you, but you were just to blind to see it. That when I knew it was time to put Steve Richards in check, I than grab him by the collar and slap his face, I said bitch what you are saying don't sound right, just don't sound right at all, I slap him 4 more time and said bitch GOD make Adam and Eve, not Adam and Steve, I than threw him on the tier and stated you stay the fuck away from me. When my visit day came, Luther Stokes and Omar Roberts came over I put a contract out on Mitch Curry, I said I go to court in 3 month, handle that A.S.A.P., 2 day later Mitch Curry was found shot to death. On a Saturday I was in the rec. hall at Central Booking watching TV., a live coverage from San Antonio Texas, was talking about Bobby Johnson. Bobby Johnson have kill 3 police (Texas Ranger), and 1 Homicide Detective was on life support, and 2 more Sheriff were shot in the arm and leg. The next day it was on TV., Radio, and newspaper. They shown mug shot of Bobby Johnson and offer an reward for his arrest, the TV. Spokesman stated that Bobby Johnson had Coke, Dope, and Crack in his house, he was under Investigation for 2 years, upon searching the house. Bobby Johnson Brother Leon Johnson made a sudden move as if he was reaching for a gun, and he was shot 32 times, Bobby Johnson was not home at the time, but upon arriving home and learning about his brother demise. Bobby Johnson call it murder and he storm the police station.

On Sunday Bobby Johnson kill a couple and stole their car. On Wednesday Bobby Johnson rob and kill another white male and car jack his blue Sedan. On Friday he shot a couple killing the woman, but the man live and told police that the suspect was heading North on I-95. The TV. Stated that Bobby Johnson was armed and Dangerous he committed a string of shooting and is suspected of robbing several store and gas station. Also he a wanted Drug king-pin considering all the Drugs, Money, and Guns found in his house in Texas. Also they said Bobby Johnson make be heading To New York, D.C., or Baltimore because he has relative and he frequent them States. I said to myself no wonder I didn't see Bobby Johnson since we graduate from (102) Elementary School, I also knew he was a bad ass from grade school, but nothing prepared me for this. I tried to go to the court-yard, library, the gym, every where I went to clear my head, there were a black inmate, every where I went it was a black face present, I said to myself, there is more niggers than in a Tarzan movies, lock-up at Central Booking. Than 11 days pass I saw on TV. In the Rec. Hall that there was a big shoot out in Baltimore, 2 Baltimore City police dead, Bobby Johnson shot in the leg, stomach, and right arm and is expected to live, they also announce the capture of Bobby Johnson and the end of the masses manhunt. 3 weeks later Bobby Johnson came over Central Booking. I was glad to see my old friend, he told me his lawyer invoke the American Constitutional amendment VIII (8). And the Declaration of Rights. Art. 25. And got him a bail but it was 6 million dollars and it have to be paid in full. I said that not a bail that a mother-fucking ransom, 1 than said they must think you're (Lee Major) the 6 million dollars man, Bobby Johnson smile and said I tried to hold court but they shot me in the right arm and the gun flew into the gutter, you know one white police put his gun to my head and pull the trigger while I was down and Un-arm, but the police gun was empty, people saw that police trying to shoot me while I was down, witness stated that not right, but even if they testify what they saw it won't help me none, all I know whitey is a bitch with his shit. I will be extradited back to Texas where the States Attorney is seeking the Death penalty, also Baltimore Prosecutor are seeking the death penalty. The police said they won't mind using "old Smokey" (the electric chair) for this case. Bobby Johnson said they also stated they won't use a mask. Just pull the switch and watch his eyes pop out, smoke come from his ears, nose, eyes and head and watch as his head and brain sizzle. The slain officer father whom was a Captain of the Baltimore Eastern District Police force said he would not even wear a mask, he want Bobby Johnson to see the pain, hurt, loss and hate in his eyes. Consider all the white people he kill the last thing he would see is a white face before he go to hell. Bobby Johnson than said that white police captain was so mad he turn pinkish red, they turn tan when the sun stay on them, with-out make-up on (TV.) they look pale, they turn purple when bruise, they turn blue when cold or dead, some of them even have green and yellow vein. And they got a nerve to call us Color People I thought to myself Bobby Johnson is Racist, Bias, and Prejudice. Because our people are even worst, in the Hood it not a white person finger on the trigger, or doing drive-by or calling each other Niggers. I never ran from the Ku-Klux-Klan but I did from a black man. From that day on I stay away From Bobby Johnson. He knew what he was getting into down in Texas. Also I know Texas is the states that executed more inmate than any other State. Than my court day came and because Mitch Curry was dead, and he was their Key witness, I beat all the Murder charges against me, but they use a make up call, they convicted me on a drugs charge and a theft charge because possession of that stolen bullet. I was sentence to 10 years in prison. The year 2000 I when to prison, I was in my 7 prison, it was all around the world the same song (Digital Underground). Every prison I when to some body try to kill me. The warden put me in (P.C.) protective custody. They said we don't want you in population. After I was sent out of 2 more prison. A Hagerstown Detective stated you know Paul King II? I said yeah he dead, the Detective said yes, but his father was not. He was a big kingpin, he was responsible for a lot of unsolved drug related murder, I said you use the word was as if it is a past tense. The detective said well when the big boy heard Paul king was under investigation and we were going to make an arrest, they had him hit. He was found in his car with a bullet to the head. Now the contract on your life is now lifted. I finish my time in peace. 2003 Bobby Johnson was executed in Texas. Steve Richards was serving a 4 consecutive life terms. I came home off the 10 years bid',. Maurice Collins had Latrobe Project lock down, out of all the strip I use to had, Latrobe project was the most luxurious and profitable. My little brother Luther Stokes and that ugly black nigger Omar Roberts were still around. Me and Andrew Mason gather up all the old crew. Me, Sonny, Andrew Mason, Troy Clark, Douglas Vilar, and Jonathan Allen were listen to rap music on the radio. The deejay announced that this new female rap star Paula Sweet, was coming to Baltimore and if you could name her Debut CD. You get to meet and greet her at dinner. I said shit I want to meet, greet, beat, eat, and freak her. Than we got into this little discussion, Andrew mason try to tell me that rap-per Hard-Dee was all that, I told him 50 Cent was the man, than Douglas Vilar and Jonathan Allen stated they like Hard-Dee too. I said he not hard the lyric he spit out is softer than funeral music. Than the crew gave me a fat envelope containing 7 thousand dollars. I than call Lynn Cartwright, she was one of the many girl that stay in contact with me throughout my incarceration. I called her that night and told her far as money and my penis I'm long, strong, and got it going on and I want to shoot a load of happy juice in her face. So we met at the Holiday Inn, and I spend half of the 7 grand my crew gave to me when I came home. So now that I back in the swing of things but no matter how I look at thing, I had to have Latrobe Project back. Latrobe was my baby. Now Maurice Collins have control of it, so I went to him and I said you know Latrobe is mine. Maurice Collins said that was than this is now. I said Maurice Collins may-be you're tire from working on all that electronic, physic, science, and chemistry. He said Dave you don't have no understanding. Than he said Dave you think who ever ain't with you is against you. He said but Dave, I said what ever. Than I said next time we meet it is friend or enemy. Than 2 day later when I saw him we just started shooting at one another, the guy Dragon smith that was with Maurice Collins was kill. The next day Maurice Collins ambush our car and kill Sonny and Prince. 4 days later I ambush Maurice Collins Black Lexus killing Big Bear whom was driving. Maurice Collins escape un-harm. Maurice Collins never forgave, forgive, or forget, he was a mean, treacherous, and vicious murderer, in this we were evenly matched. Than one day I call all my Boys together and said we got to get Maurice Collins. First I want his two top Lieutenant killed, Benfield and Cabrera. With-in 2 day Benfield was found shot to death in his truck, Cabrera was shot to death as he came from a Down-Town Night Club. 3 days later Maurice Collins struck back, a car came flying down the street dumping bullet on Me, Drake Thomas, Philip and Jack Leister. Drake Thomas was shot in the throat, neck, and chest he died before he hit the ground, Jack Leister was shot in both legs and he turn to run for cover he was than shot 3 time in the back and once in the neck. We return fire but we miss, the following day I sent Maurice Collins an answer to that, I had his two Brother slain Victor and Tyrone Collins. Than I call a meeting to get rid of Maurice Collins once and for all. We had our meeting at 9:00 Am. Fuzi, Andrew Mason, and my Chauffeur Tyson Zolenas shook my hand and said since you are staying to wrap things up. We will be back 11:30 Am. We are going to grab a bite to eat. So the 3 of them left and got in my brand new Cadillac Escalade Truck, than I heard the big blast it broke out all the window of our meeting Hall and I was knock to the floor, as I got up to look out the window at the wreck and burn up truck. I knew deep in my heart that was meant for me. Also all I could think of was Maurice Collins Electronic, science, physics, and chemistry classes finally pay off. 2 week later Jack Leister was still in the Hospital, the Doctor said he will be confine to a wheel chair. Now all the other Drug Dealer wanted Me and Maurice Collins to squash our beef. One day I was home listen to Raw Bass (pain and joy) I play and listen to the part over and over again, we use to be friend now we foe ask me why 1 don't know, may-be the pain, envy, or the money. Maurice Collins sent word he wanted to talk, so I came to him. As he approach me. All I could think about was this is

64

the man who kill children, killed little Paul King III, and a lot of my friends and comrade. Maurice Collins said Dave man we use to be friend, you plug me in, I had your back in the line of fire. I said fuck that. I ain't got no understanding, I don't want to hear it. I than said you either step down or I will put you down. We back away from each other, 2 month went by than one morning Maurice Collins came out of his house to go to work. As he walk to his car, I step from the screen door of the house next door to his house, and I crept up behind him, put the gun behind his head and whisper Goodbye and pull the trigger. Now that the war was over, the Project was all mine. Now that I had Latrobe all the Drug Dealer in Baltimore came to pay tribute. Luther Stokes and Omar Roberts re-join me, we started getting money. One day we were down Crecida's by Old Town Mall, inside the Club they had an old rap song on M.C. Shannon and Marley Mar (Brooklyn Bridge) I like the part " Before you enter this club you were frisk before you when in." we use to go upstairs open the back window throw a rope, shoe-string, or string out of the window and heist and pull our gun up, on one particular day this guy bump up to me, I look at him real hard, he got nasty. Luther Stokes and Omar Roberts was there. I told the guy be cool fool, he stated fuck all of you. I said I'm not responsible for what my Boys do, the guy still ran his mouth, I turn my head I heard the guns go off, every body started running out of the Club. 5 days later I was at the Club Odells (you know if you belong). Odells was the best Club on North Ave. I dance for a while and than I took a shit and wipe my ass with fifths and hundreds dollars Bill, the legend grew I Got so much money I shit out Money and I `m made out of money. I took a couple of sophisticated older female to some oldie but good-ie concert, we went to the Dells concert we listen to the Dells sing give your baby a standing ovation, always together, bring back the love of yesterday. One time I took this female to a big concert Barry White You're the first, the last, my everything. The delegation "Oh Honey" Lamont Dozier "The Fish ain't Bittin" Jermaine Jackson "You like me don't you" Freda Payne 'All that left is a band of gold" Al Green "Look what you done for me". As time when on we were getting paid in full. One day I was looking at all the photo of Me, my gang, other drug dealers, and me and a lot of female. my father said Dave you got Charisma, so I said I will throw a big party to bring all the Drug Dealers together. I felt kind of scare, I never knew fear like this before, I knew something bad was going to happen to me. My father said it was a Power move. I was thinking to myself, one thing for sure no black man a live ever try to bring such a big power move. At this time I was beefing with a North-East Baltimore Drug gang. I said after the party we will take care of them. I than made a hit list. And also I made a list of all the people I wanted to show up at the party I was throwing. I told Douglas Vilar to make the list. Some sort of way this stupid nigger got the list confuse, my little Brother, and Omar Roberts was on the hit list. This was unknown to me until Omar Roberts came into my sister room and stabbed me five times, and put me in Maryland Shock Trauma Hospital at University Hospital on Greene Street. From Shock Trauma, I told my friends to get everybody together to find out and discuss what happen. They stated we will talk but your brother got to go. I said No. they said your little brother just wanted to be like (you) Dave. Some people said no wonder he was name Luther because he Lucifer. I said no, my Grandmother and mother warn me never to trust a dark skin nigger, and Omar Roberts was a real Dark skinned Brother. When I went to Court I found out why Omar Roberts stabbed me up. The Judge stated if any thing happen to Omar Roberts, I would get life in prison. My mind was under a lot of pressure. I could not kill Omar Roberts and now people wanted my Little brother dead. And at this point I was beefing heavy with this North –East gang. All this death, hate, envy, pain, and destruction since 1965 and since I been in the drug game. Too Much, Too Soon. I than left Maryland Shock Trauma Hospital, I hit the street and I saw one of the North-East drug Dealer, I ran him in the house, than I saw his son so I grab him and put the gun to his head and I ask the father to come out of the house, but the father refuse to come out of the house. So 1 let the child go and I ran because I can't, would not, and could not kill or hurt a child. It was just a ploy to get the father to come out of the house. I truly believe if you kill or hurt one of GOD little Children GOD will Blacken and Darken your Soul. You won't even sense, hear, or feel some-body creeping up on you. I finish off the rest of the North-East gang. The police lock me up and said take an evaluation or face Criminal charges. I said to myself Life a bitch than you die, and life a bitch; here to day gone tomorrow. And than I said all I been through, it just should not end like this. I was sent to Crownsville State Hospital for 4 days. After that I was release, a lot of people turn their back and said I was finish, A use to be, and some said I was wash up.(a has been) I came home me *and* my little brother Luther Stokes became as one. You hurt him, you hurt me. Luther Stokes explain that Douglas Vilar and the person that stabbed me was no longer above ground. So me and Luther Stokes walked the street together, so everybody could see we were one. I hug Luther and told him we are brother and soldier from the womb to the tomb. It was Dec. 25, 2004 A Christmas morning Renee Simms drop by, she said she know every thing I been Through, and she forgive me. We listen to some Christmas song, Carla Thomas; Gee Whiz, it Christmas, The Emotions; What do the lonely do at Christmas, Paul fat daddy Johnson; Fat Daddy (Santa Claus), Santa Baby; Rev. Run and the Christmas all Star. Some day at Christmas; Stevie Wonder. Renee Simms made me Promise that I would go to Church with her soon, than she left. One day a guy march down on Luther and Luther open fire killing him in broad day light. Luther got a big sentence for that murder. My brother crime was in the newspaper. Also I read about this black man name Kippy Armstrong getting 7 life sentences. Me, Herbert Kelly, and Jonathan Allen wonder if it was because his skin was kiss by nature sun. Herbert Kelly than stated Kippy Armstrong was his first cousin, and it look like Herbert Kelly was about to cry, I said go ahead and cry. I said it take a big man to cry, and even a bigger man to laugh at him. They both laugh. I said laughter is the best medicine and it is good for you, than I said but not if you laugh at the wrong person. They both laugh again. Time flew on it was now March 2005. And I was ready to receive, one morning I pick up the Bible and I saw the name David in it. (King David) "Psalm". Than I stated all I been through and I'm still alive. So I got all my friends together and told them about it. They stated you're meant to be a Player, Drug Dealer, Big Baller, and Shot Caller. I said no. the street don't love no body, and like John Gotti said in this Drug business you wonder who going to nail you first the Government or your best friend. I 'm on this live and let live tip. I said we can agree to disagree, and I don't care if you see blue and I see green. I thank GOD you could see. They stated Dave we are ready to go home. I said see you all later. As I sat alone, I ponder and wonder and I said to myself No matter how much you try to do what is right there are people who won't understand, acknowledge, or accept you. But l count it all Joy. Just enjoy your cross because Jesus enjoy on the Cross. These and many thought ran around in my head and mind. I play my radio and Cameo; Why have I lost you. Was on it. I like the part. Tonight

I 'm a lonely man but tomorrow I will be a King. I thought about Renee Simms and I felt to sleep. The next day I told my friends and associate I plan to throw a big party to celebrate that I'm stepping down, 2 month later all the Drug Dealers from East, West, North, and South Baltimore came, also we have some out of Towner. It was a lot of female there, also Jonathan Allen,, Herbert Kelly, Troy Clark, Naomi Washington, Philip and Jack Leister. Jack was in the wheel chair, but he still came. Every body was there. I address the audience and said to all the men out in the audience, I know you know there was some Helleva Niggers both friends and foe, both dead and alive that came out of this Drug Thing of our. I than said to all the women; I know you all have seen Niggers come and go in this Drug Thing of our. Always remember many are call, but chosen are few. When all the guns goes off and the smoke clear up, and he who left standing is the real winner. We than play music and party for hours. Some of the music the D-J play was Salt-n- Pepa; Shoot. Lil-kim, Biggie Smalls, Mase; Crush on you. Nonchalant; 5' °clock. Too Short; The Ghetto. P.M. Dawn; Set adrift on memory bliss. LL cool J; Around the way girl. Onyx; Slam. Queen Latifah; U.N.I.T.Y., Fugees; Ready or not. Sybil; Don't make me over. Big Daddy Kane; ain't no half steppin'. Marvin Gaye; God is my friend. Marvin Gaye; What's happening brother. I told the D.J. to keep on playing Cream by Wu-tang Clan, Because back in 1982 1 went to Jail/Prison for an arm robbery at the age 15, came home and when all out with a Drug gang. Than I have the D.J. play the slow version of Open arms by Tina Turner, and "Again" by Faith Evans, because I Ponder and wonder if I would do it all Again, would I join the drug game again, I said to myself if I had to do it all again probably not. Since I was changing, getting in touch with my Spiritual side. I had the D.J. play Sinner Prayer by Deitrick Haddon. I made another speech and I said I love all of you and I love all the Comrade that dead and gone. Than I had the D-j. play Diana Ross and the Supremes last fare-well hit. Some day we will be together, and I shout some day we will all be together. And I made my grand exit from the party amid handshake, hugs, kisses, good wishes, and tears. 2 days later I when to visit my mother and family, I couldn't bear facing them with blood on my hand, that why I waited until I changed. 4 days later Me and Renee Simms went to her Family Church. It was a good and bless day at the church they play Yolanda Adams; The battle is the Lord. Yolanda Adams; Through the storm. And Renee

Simms say she have a request can you play Helen Baylor; Can you reach my friend. And I want to dedicate this to my Friend David Stokes. They play the song and than service was over. 2 week later I gave my life to Jesus and God. And I was Baptized in the name of Jesus, God and the Holy Ghost. The church help me get an apartment in the Northwood section, I talk to some City Hall Council Man and Women. They invited me to a few of their Christmas party held in the World Trade Center. Also I was an Extra in the HBO show the Wire and the Head of states. I did an Interview on Fox 45 news. Also now I met a lot of new interesting female and some new male buddy. I know I'm some body because God didn't make no junk. Now I have some favor Verse and it all fit in with my life story. Also I wrote this song and poem title I been running too long, and I wrote a rap song called Here Come Shorty. Truly God and Jesus In-spire me to write this book, song, and poem. The Muslim said if you know who you're, you won't do the things you do. I had to love, respect, and cherish every day and today because it a gift from God that why they call it the Present. Also I had to fear God and get right with God. Right to this very day I pray and go to church, I was one of those guys you could not tell nothing, I had to learn the hard way. Now I have Jesus, Virgin Mary, The Holy Ghost, and God in my life and he's the only way. From me to you, get out while you can. It is not worth your life, freedom, mind, heart, or soul, or is it?

GOD IS REAL: I CAN IDENTIFY

Galatians 6:7 Be not deceived; GOD is not mocked: for what so ever a man soweth that shall he also reap.

Proverb 4:1 The way of the wicked is as darkness, they know not at what they stumble.

Psalm 140: 11 Let not an evil person be established in the earth: evil shall hunt the violent man to overthrow him.

Proverb 17:17 A friend loveth at all times and a brother is born for adversity.

Romans 1:28 And even as they did not like to retain GOD in their knowledge, God gave them over to a reprobate mind, to do those things which are not convenient.

Psalm 142:4 I looked on my right hand, and beheld, but there was no man that would know me: refuge failed me; no man cared for my soul.

Isaiah 53:1-3 Who hath believed our report? And to whom is the arm of the Lord revealed? **2.** For he shall grow up before him as a tender plant, and as a root out of a dry ground: he hath no form nor comeliness; and when we shall see him, there is no beauty that we should desire him. **3.** He is despised and rejected of men; a man of sorrows, and acquainted with grief: and we hid as it were our faces from him; he was despised, and we esteemed him not.

GOD IS GOOD: I CAN IDENTIFY

Proverb 9:10 The fear of the Lord is the beginning of wisdom: and the knowledge of the holy is understanding.

Proverb 9:9 Give instruction to a wise man, and he will be yet wiser: teach a just man, and he will increase in learning.

Psalm 40:1 I waited patiently for the Lord; and he inclined unto me, and heard my cry.

Psalm 40:2 He brought me up also out of an horrible pit, out of the miry clay and set my foot upon a rock, and established my goings.

Psalm 84:11 For the Lord GOD is a sun and shield: the Lord will give grace and glory: no good things will he withhold from them that walk up rightly.

Psalm 37:4 Delight thyself also in the Lord; and he shall give thee the desires of thine heart.

Proverb 21:21 He that followeth after righteousness, and mercy findeth life, righteousness, and honour.

I BEEN RUNNING TOO LONG (Song/Poem)

Yes, I been running too long, yes I been running too long. Jesus make this song sweet and strong for all the old and young. Because I been running too long. I ask the Lord up above is there any one true that I could love. There has been many that came and went, now my heart have a burning and yearning desire to put up a fence. After so much hurt, pain and rain, I just about went Insane. I need you Jesus, the baby, the good, old and poor will travel through heavens door. It's a fight to be spiritually right. But I was knocked down, hit rock bottom, woke up and saw the spiritual light.

Too much, Too soon. So I gave my life to the Lord. After so many trials and tribulations it's time for dedication to Jesus, I went through hell in jail with no bail, I looked for Jesus in prison and I only Found (Jes-ys). With no uncertain term I demonstrate to a degree that I could use guns, knives, and Tai-Bow now I carry only the Bible, oh yes I been Running too long, yes this old heart have been running too long.

As I slip, crawl, struggle and stumble down life lonely highway running a long a street paved with pain, Fear, destruction, and tears. But Jesus shown me he's real. I know he love me every hour, second, and minute. ON this lonely byway and highway I will stop at a store and get some new tennis, because I been running for a minute. And this is a good song because I been running too long. Yes, I been running too long.

HERE COMES SHORTY (Rap Lyrics)

1. Here come Shorty five times bigger than Steven, been clocking on the corner all that evening.

2. Once brag he had shipments of dope, crack, and coke flowing from coast to coast, making connections from his airplane or his million dollar luxury boat.

3. One day Shorty got popped by an outrageous cop, sitting in jail with a ransom instead of a bail. No love in jail was worth AIDS, losing his head playing chess or spades. Now time for release he's back out on the mean streets.

4. Gun in his dip, hand on his gold prick everywhere he went knowing full well he could get his dick sucked for three dollars or sixty cents.

5. Shorty felt ill knowing he had to kill to stay strong and make that dollar dollar bill, while keeping it real all the time playing his girl Jill.

6. Separation brings appreciation, now him and his girl is apart, tears and emotion is falling from his heart, he knew he would lose her from the very start.

7. If there is a God above, why all this killing and no love, I go hard and buck, because I don't give a fuck.

8. Pandemonium spill, whom will Shorty kill to stay strong and make that dollar dollar bill.

9. Now as time dwell, slip and pass. Shorty got shot twice in the chest and once in the ass. Now his dream is at an end, he's wondering was it an enemy or a friend, who was trying to make sure; Here Come Shorty never rise again.

HE THAT HATH EARS WILL LISTEN

I would like to introduce them to read a Book, and a Chess Game. Read a book, you will get hook, and you might not have to be a crook. Chess Game and the drug game is a way of life. But if they're taught how to play chess which is a thinking man game, it will set there mind to thinking, and it will put their mind in a thinking mode. They will be able to out smart, out think, out maneuver, out manipulate, an anticipate the dope man next move. For example the drug dealer come up to them and said I got a fresh pair of Jordan tennis and $575.00 just for you. If your mind is in a thinking mode you will question yourself because nothing free, than you would ask yourself why me. It use to take a whole village to raise a child, now it take a whole community. Now it is no Unity in the Community, let get Churches involve, I mean deeply involve. East and west Baltimore is hit the hardest, because all of this shooting, killing, drugs, AIDS, and teenage pregnancy. It is like the wild wild west. And there is no rest in the West, no peace in the East. Baltimore City use to be call Charm City, now it is call Harm City, they call Baltimore city B-more-careful, one has to be more careful in the street of Baltimore city. Here are some what will you do Scenario for the youth of Baltimore city. If you are in a small prison cell with a inmate whom is real black, ugly with a mean mug, 380 pound of solid muscle with no neck, looking like a cross between Arnold Schwarzenegger, Ray Lewis and Mike Tyson. With a knife in one hand and his penis in the other hand. Most will say I will kill him. The judge and jury will ask you what was you doing with a knife? You and I both know a gun and a knife is for protection. But that did not stop them from convicting you on the street when you use a gun. Another what will you do? You committed a murder and did 17 years on a 45 years prison sentence, while you were in prison you saw that you didn't want to be a thug any more, also you're now much older and wiser, don't want to be with the in crowd no longer, so after a while your homeboys (dawgs) goes their own way, some even now sling drugs with the family of the people you slain, also at the trial 17 years ago was the slain victim family he got 4 brothers, 7 uncles, 3 sons, whom are now grown up and in the drug game. They were also making finger handgun (gesture) at you in the court room, now here you go 17 years later with a homicide, handgun violation with two drug conviction, the third will result in 25 no parole, you have no real money, you're a convicted felon which in return mean you can't get a good job, and you can't carry a fire arm (gun) than you're release back in the same hoods(area) that you kill the guy, you see GOD forgive and forget but man don't you will see there is nothing left but memory and enemy. Even if you do luck up and move or your family move. You must remember Baltimore is a small place, also they say this world is a small place, but even smaller when somebody gunning for you. Some people will say I will put it in JESUS (GOD'S) hands. But what about going to church and putting things in God's hands before you are faced with one of these Scenario. Also look at the big picture where will you be 10 years from now?

DAVID (DAVE) STOKES

I am a blessed and truly lucky man. I made history as the first black ex-drug dealer that had an interview on national TV. The first of my kind to tell his story on TV. And have my 15 minutes of fame, and I am not doing a lot of prison time, not shot up, not dead or not on drugs, and not facing no prison or jail time. All the other drug dealers or ex-drug dealers are only in the newspaper. I give it all to God, if you got eyes you should see my life story. Please order this video tape.

David Stokes
Tuesday; August 16, 2005
Fox 45 news
10:00 PM News
Baltimore, Maryland Call 410-467-5595
410-446-5753
410-467-5397
or call 1-800-969-8845 for a copy of the video
News reporter; Keith Daniels

DAVE

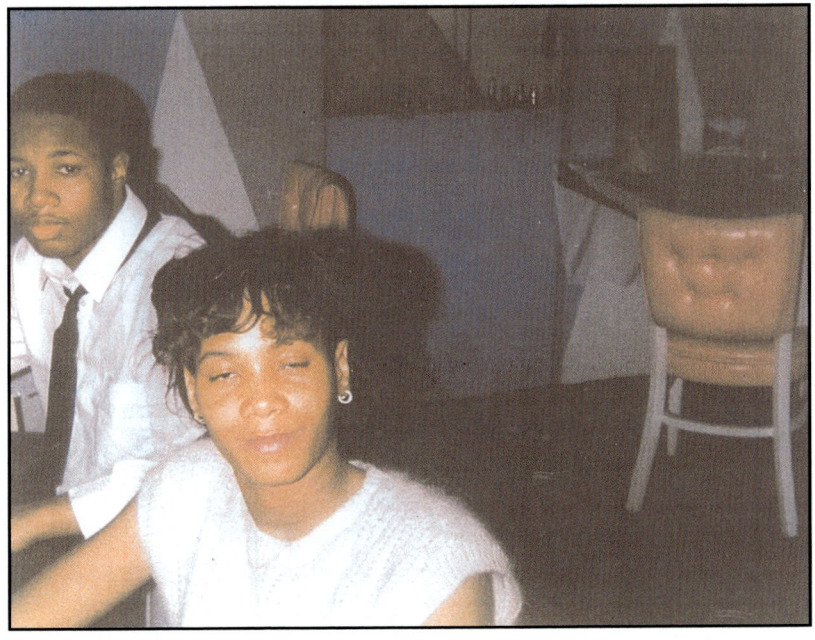

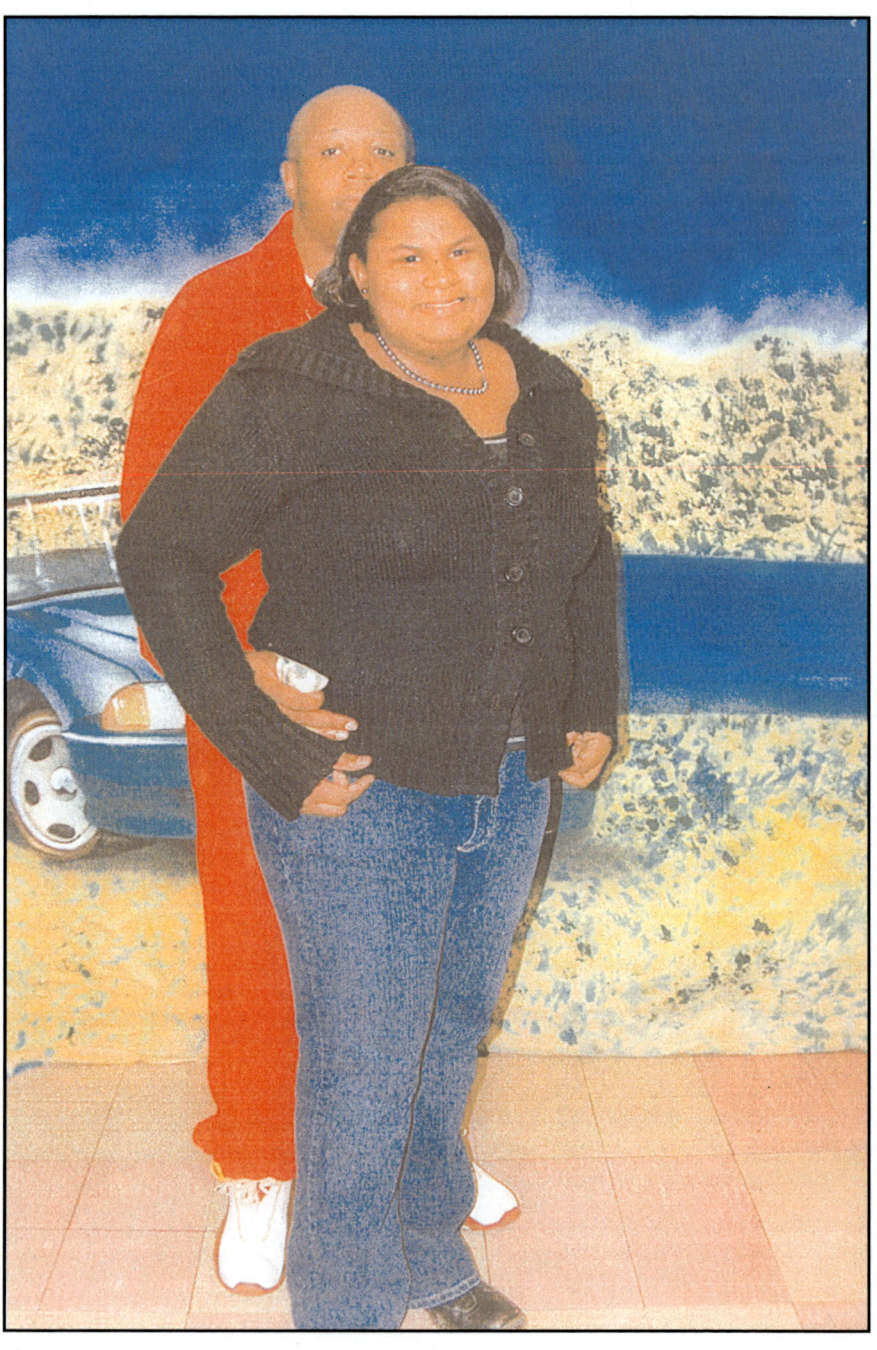

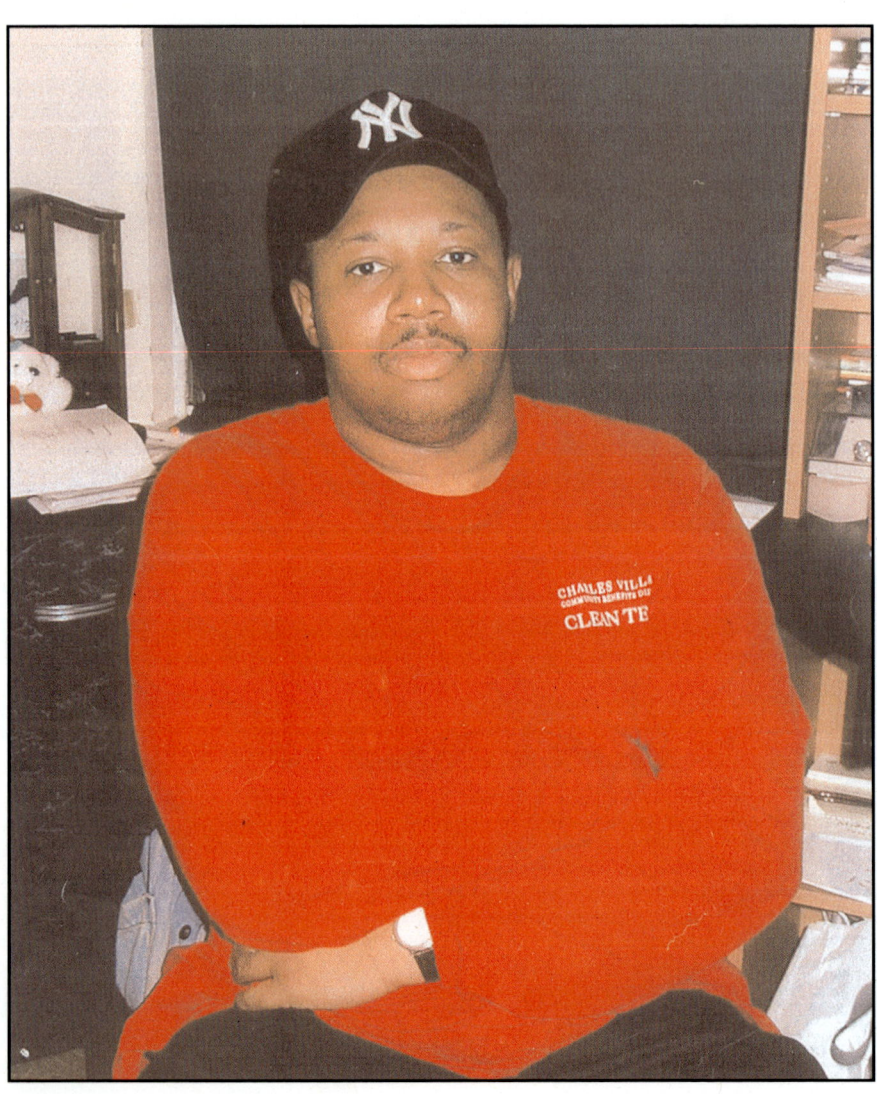

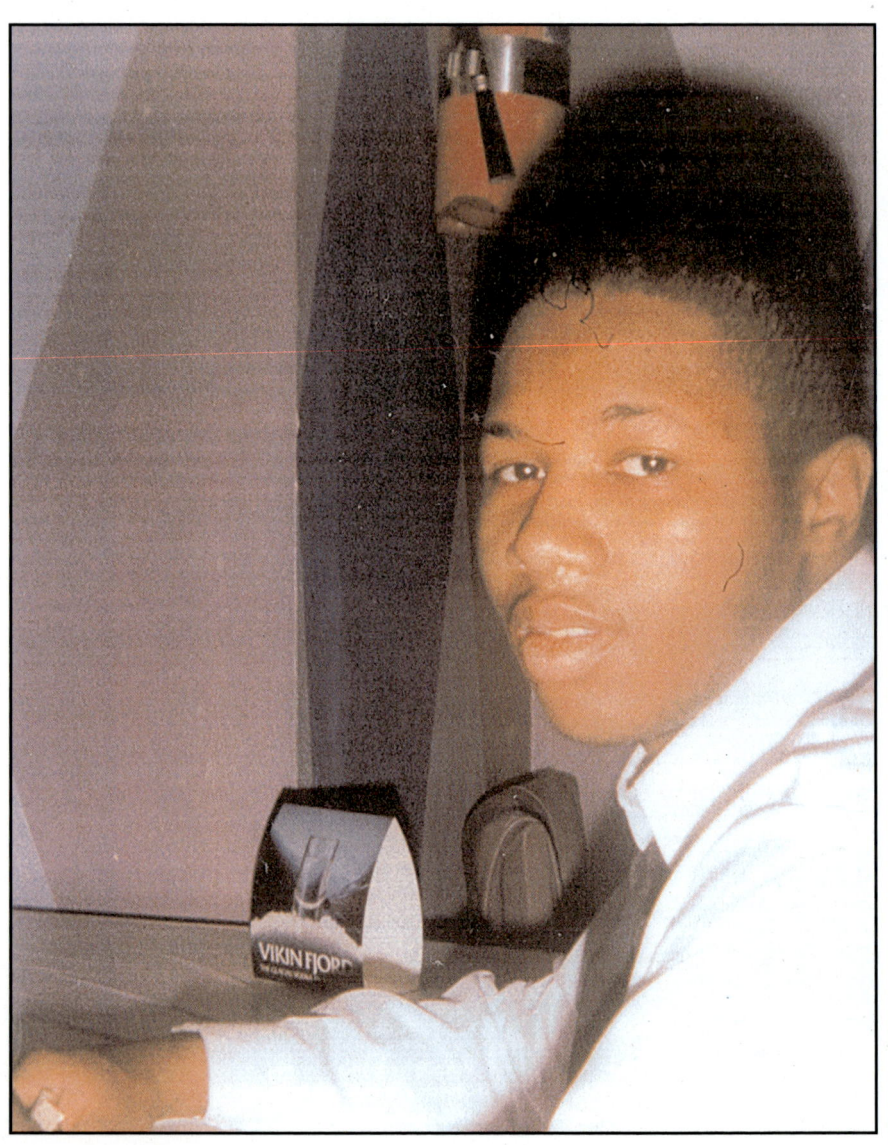

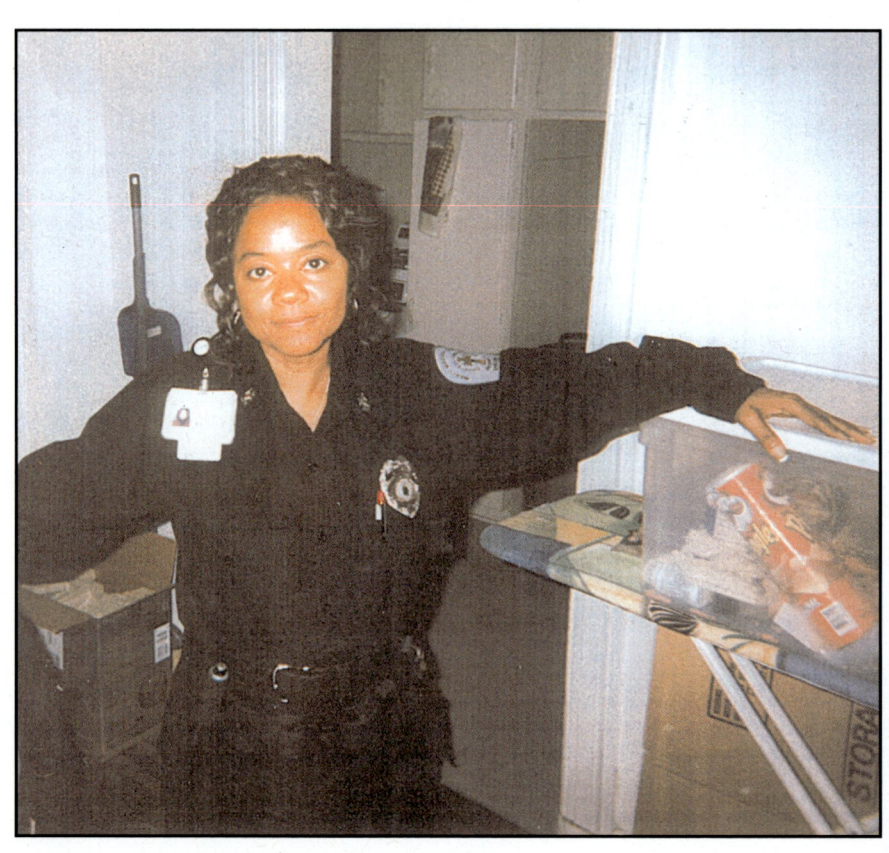